D0182737

OVE · MARRIAGE · LOSS · JOURNEYS

FIRST LOVE

FIRST LOVE

EDITED BY

Paul Bailey

J. M. Dent London

First published in Great Britain in 1997
by J. M. Dent

A CIP catalogue record for this book is available
from the British Library.

ISBN 0 460 87929 4

Typeset at The Spartan Press Ltd,
Lymington, Hants
Set in 10/13pt Photina
Printed in Great Britain by Clays Ltd,
St Ives plc

J. M. Dent

Weidenfeld & Nicolson
The Orion Publishing Group Ltd
Orion House
5 Upper Saint Martin's Lane
London, WC2H 9EA

CONTENTS

INTRODUCTION

'The magic of first love is our ignorance that it can ever end', wrote Benjamin Disraeli. This short anthology has been designed to reflect something of that magical condition, as well as the joys, torments and sorrows that are its usual accompaniments. The book opens and closes with a Shakespeare sonnet – the first a celebration of incomparable youthful beauty; the second a brief hymn to the triumph of love over time and physical decay. In between there are lovers galore, from the familiar to the virtually unknown. They appear in no particular or chronological order, for the reason that the subject itself is timeless. John Clare's lines 'And then my blood rushed to my face/And took my eyesight quite away' are applicable to somebody somewhere at this very minute, and will continue to be apt into infinity.

Many of the poems included here are not as widely known as they ought to be. I am thinking of Giles Fletcher's wondrous 'Wooing Song', in which the future clergyman lets rip with a lyrical vengeance: 'Love no med'cine can appease/He burns the fishes in the seas', and the several anonymous masterpieces, such as 'Donal Og' in Lady Gregory's translation and the haunting ballad 'Andrew Lammie' which is still sung in Scotland. I have set these, and others, alongside the justifiably famous, by Andrew Marvell, Sir Philip Sidney, Robert Burns and Elizabeth Barrett Browning.

I am conscious that Dido's unhealthy passion for Aeneas is her second infatuation but – in John Dryden's rendering of Virgil – she could be any besotted slave to a heroic man. I should also reveal that 'Appletreewick' by W. H. Auden was written when the poet was sixteen and enamoured of his friend Robert Medley, who later became a painter of quiet and subtle distinction. (The Medley family lived in Appletreewick, in the Yorkshire dales.) And in the scene I have chosen from *As You Like It*, Rosalind is pretending to be a young man pretending to be Rosalind – the better to teach Orlando the art of courtship.

No further explanations seem necessary. *First Love* has been compiled with the prospect of delight in mind. That Teresa of Avila's first and last love is the God she calls her 'spouse' and that poor Joe Ackerley came to prefer the companionship of an Alsatian bitch to the discontents of the bedroom – these are statements of loving fact, even so. 'Love doth make the Heav'ns to move,/And the sun doth burn in love.'

FIRST LOVE

WILLIAM SHAKESPEARE

Sonnet 18

Shall I compare thee to a summer's day?
Thou art more lovely and more temperate:
Rough winds do shake the darling buds of May,
And summer's lease hath all too short a date:
Sometime too hot the eye of heaven shines,
And often is his gold complexion dimmed,
And every fair from fair sometime declines,
By chance, or nature's changing course untrimmed:
But thy eternal summer shall not fade,
Nor lose possession of that fair thou ow'st,
Nor shall death brag thou wand'rest in his shade,
When in eternal lines to time thou grow'st,
    So long as men can breathe or eyes can see,
    So long lives this, and this gives life to thee.

JOHN MILTON

from *Paradise Lost*

(Eve speaks to Adam)
With thee conversing I forget all time,
All seasons and their change, all please alike.
Sweet is the breath of morn, her rising sweet,
With charm of earliest birds; pleasant the sun
When first on this delightful land he spreads
His orient beams, on herb, tree, fruit, and flower,
Glistring with dew; fragrant the fertile earth
After soft showers; and sweet the coming on
Of grateful evening mild, then silent night
With this her solemn bird and this fair moon,
And these the gems of heav'n, her starry train:
But neither breath of morn when she ascends
With charm of earliest birds, nor rising sun
On this delightful land, nor herb, fruit, flower,
Glistring with dew, nor fragrance after showers,
Nor grateful evening mild, nor silent night
With this her solemn bird, nor walk by moon,
Or glittering starlight without thee is sweet.

SAPPHO

Mother, I cannot mind my wheel;
　My fingers ache, my lips are dry;
Oh! if you felt the pain I feel!
　But oh, who ever felt as I!

translated by
Walter Savage Landor

THE BIBLE

from 'The Song of Solomon'

I am the rose of Sharon, and the lily of the valleys.

As the lily among thorns, so is my love among the daughters.

As the apple tree among the trees of the wood, so is my beloved among the sons. I sat down under his shadow with great delight, and his fruit was sweet to my taste.

He brought me to the banqueting house, and his banner over me was love.

Stay me with flagons, comfort me with apples: for I am sick of love.

His left hand is under my head, and his right hand doth embrace me.

I charge you, O ye daughters of Jerusalem, by the roes, and by the hinds of the field, that ye stir not up, nor awake my love, till he please.

The voice of my beloved! behold, he cometh leaping upon the mountains, skipping upon the hills.

My beloved is like a roe or a young hart: behold, he standeth behind our wall, he looketh forth at the windows, showing himself through the lattice.

My beloved spake, and said unto me, Rise up, my love, my fair one, and come away.

For, lo, the winter is past, the rain is over and gone;

The flowers appear on the earth; the time of the singing of birds is come, and the voice of the turtle is heard in our land:

The fig tree putteth forth her green figs, and the vines with the tender grape give a good smell. Arise, my love, my fair one, and come away.

O my dove, that art in the clefts of the rock, in the secret places of the stairs, let me see thy countenance, let me hear thy voice; for sweet is thy voice, and thy countenance is comely.

Take us the foxes, the little foxes, that spoil the vines: for our vines have tender grapes.

My beloved is mine, and I am his: he feedeth among the lilies.

Until the day break, and the shadows flee away, turn, my beloved, and be thou like a roe or a young hart upon the mountains of Bether.

JOHN DRYDEN

from Virgil's *Aeneid*

Sick with desire, and seeking him she loves,
From Street to Street, the raving *Dido* roves.
So when the watchful Shepherd, from the Blind,
Wounds with a random Shaft the careless Hind;
Distracted with her pain she flies the Woods,
Bounds o're the Lawn, and seeks the silent Floods;
With fruitless Care; for still the fatal Dart
Sticks in her side; and ranckles in her Heart.
And now she leads the *Trojan* Chief, along
The lofty Walls, amidst the buisie Throng;
Displays her *Tyrian* Wealth, and rising Town,
Which Love, without his Labour, makes his own.
This Pomp she shows to tempt her wand'ring Guest;
Her falt'ring Tongue forbids to speak the rest.
When Day declines, and Feasts renew the Night,
Still on his Face she feeds her famish'd sight;
She longs again to hear the Prince relate
His own Adventures, and the *Trojan* Fate:
He tells it o're and o're; but still in vain;
For still she begs to hear it, once again.
The Hearer on the Speaker's Mouth depends;

And thus the Tragick Story never ends.
    Then, when they part, when *Phoebe*'s paler Light
Withdraws, and falling Stars to Sleep invite,
She last remains, when ev'ry Guest is gone,
Sits on the Bed he press'd, and sighs alone.

WILLIAM SHAKESPEARE

❧

from *As You Like It*

ORLANDO My fair Rosalind, I come within an hour of my promise.

ROSALIND Break an hour's promise in love! He that will divide a minute into a thousand parts, and break but a part of the thousand part of a minute in the affairs of love, it may be said of him that Cupid hath clapped him o' th' shoulder, but I'll warrant him heart-whole.

ORLANDO Pardon me dear Rosalind.

ROSALIND Nay, and you be so tardy, come no more in my sight. I had as lief be wooed of a snail.

ORLANDO Of a snail?

ROSALIND Ay, of a snail. For though he comes slowly, he carries his house on his head; a better jointure I think than you make a woman. Besides, he brings his destiny with him.

ORLANDO What's that?

ROSALIND Why horns – which such as you are fain to be beholding to your wives for: but he comes armed in his fortune, and prevents the slander of his wife.

ORLANDO Virtue is no horn-maker; and my Rosalind is virtuous.

ROSALIND And I am your Rosalind.

CELIA It pleases him to call you so: but he hath a Rosalind of a better leer than you.

ROSALIND Come, woo me, woo me; for now I am in a holiday humour and like enough to consent. What would you say to me now, and I were your very very Rosalind?

ORLANDO I would kiss before I spoke.

ROSALIND Nay, you were better speak first, and when you were gravelled for lack of matter, you might take occasion to kiss. Very good orators when they are out, they will spit, and for lovers lacking – God warr'nt us! – matter, the cleanliest shift is to kiss.

ORLANDO How if the kiss be denied?

ROSALIND Then she puts you to entreaty, and there begins new matter.

ORLANDO Who could be out, being before his beloved mistress?

ROSALIND Marry that should you, if I were your mistress, or I should think my honesty ranker than my wit.

ORLANDO What, of my suit?

ROSALIND Not out of your apparel, and yet out of your suit. Am not I your Rosalind?

ORLANDO I take some joy to say you are, because I would be talking of her.

ROSALIND Well, in her person, I say I will not have you.

ORLANDO Then in mine own person, I die.

ROSALIND No, faith, die by attorney. The poor world is almost six thousand years old, and in all this time there was not any man died in his own person, videlicet, in a love-cause. Troilus had his brains dashed out with a Grecian club, yet he did what he could to die before, and he is one of the patterns of love. Leander, he would have lived many a fair year though Hero had turned nun, if it had not been for a hot mid summer night; for, good youth, he went but forth to wash him in the Hellespont, and being taken with the cramp, was drowned, and the foolish chroniclers of that age found it was Hero of Sestos. But these are all lies: men have died from time to time and worms have eaten them, but not for love.

ORLANDO I would not have my right Rosalind of this mind, for I protest her frown might kill me.

ROSALIND By this hand, it will not kill a fly. But come, now I will be your Rosalind in a more coming-on disposition; and ask me what you will, I will grant it.

ORLANDO Then love me Rosalind.

ROSALIND Yes faith will I, Fridays and Saturdays and all.

ORLANDO And wilt thou have me?

ROSALIND Ay, and twenty such.

ORLANDO What sayest thou?

ROSALIND Are you not good?

ORLANDO I hope so.

ROSALIND Why then, can one desire too much of a good thing? Come sister, you shall be the priest and marry us. Give me your hand Orlando. What do you say sister?

ORLANDO Pray thee marry us.

CELIA I cannot say the words.

ROSALIND You must begin, 'Will you Orlando——'

CELIA Go to. Will you Orlando have to wife this Rosalind?

ORLANDO I will.

ROSALIND Ay, but when?

ORLANDO Why now, as fast as she can marry us.

ROSALIND Then you must say 'I take thee Rosalind for wife.'

ORLANDO I take thee Rosalind for wife.

ROSALIND I might ask you for your commission; but I do

take thee Orlando for my husband. There's a girl goes before the priest, and certainly a woman's thought runs before her actions.

ORLANDO So do all thoughts, they are winged.

ROSALIND Now tell me how long you would have her, after you have possessed her?

ORLANDO For ever, and a day.

ROSALIND Say a day, without the ever. No, no, Orlando, men are April when they woo, December when they wed. Maids are May when they are maids, but the sky changes when they are wives. I will be more jealous of thee than a Barbary cock-pigeon over his hen, more clamorous than a parrot against rain, more new-fangled than an ape, more giddy in my desires than a monkey. I will weep for nothing, like Diana in the fountain, and I will do that when you are disposed to be merry. I will laugh like a hyen, and that when thou art inclined to sleep.

ORLANDO But will my Rosalind do so?

ROSALIND By my life, she will do as I do.

C. P. CAVAFY

'In the Evening'

It wouldn't have lasted long anyway –
years of experience make that clear.
But Fate did put an end to it a bit abruptly.
It was soon over, that wonderful life.
Yet how strong the scents were,
what a magnificent bed we lay in,
what pleasures we gave our bodies.

An echo from my days of indulgence,
an echo from those days came back to me,
something of the fire of the young life we shared:
I picked up a letter again,
read it over and over till the light faded.

Then, sad, I went out on to the balcony,
went out to change my thoughts at least by seeing
something of this city I love,
a little movement in the streets, in the shops.

ST JOHN OF THE CROSS

Upon a gloomy night,
With all my cares to loving ardours flushed,
(O venture of delight!)
With nobody in sight
I went abroad when all my house was hushed.

In safety, in disguise,
In darkness up the secret stair I crept,
(O happy enterprise)
Concealed from other eyes
When all my house at length in silence slept.

Upon that lucky night
In secrecy, inscrutable to sight,
I went without discerning
And with no other light
Except for that which in my heart was burning.

It lit and led me through
More certain than the light of noonday clear
To where One waited near
Whose presence well I knew,
There where no other presence might appear.

Oh night that was my guide!
Oh darkness dearer than the morning's pride,
Oh night that joined the lover
To the beloved bride
Transfiguring them each into the other.

Within my flowering breast
Which only for himself entire I save
He sank into his rest
And all my gifts I gave
Lulled by the airs with which the cedars wave.

Over the ramparts fanned
While the fresh wind was fluttering his tresses,
With his serenest hand
My neck he wounded, and
Suspended every sense with its caresses.

Lost to myself I stayed
My face upon my lover having laid
From all endeavour ceasing:
And all my cares releasing
Threw them amongst the lilies there to fade.

translated by
Roy Campbell

D. H. LAWRENCE

'Green'

The dawn was apple-green,
   The sky was green wine held up in the sun,
The moon was a golden petal between.

She opened her eyes, and green
   They shone, clear like flowers undone
For the first time, now for the first time seen.

JOHN CLARE

'First Love'

I ne'er was struck before that hour
    With love so sudden and so sweet,
Her face it bloomed like a sweet flower
    And stole my heart away complete.
My face turned pale as deadly pale,
    My legs refused to walk away,
And when she looked, what could I ail?
    My life and all seemed turned to clay.

And then my blood rushed to my face
    And took my eyesight quite away,
The trees and bushes round the place
    Seemed midnight at noonday.
I could not see a single thing,
    Words from my eyes did start –
They spoke as chords do from the string,
    And blood burnt round my heart.

Are flowers the winter's choice?
    Is love's bed always snow?
She seemed to hear my silent voice,

Not love's appeals to know.
I never saw so sweet a face
    As that I stood before.
My heart has left its dwelling-place
    And can return no more.

CHARLES OF ORLEANS

My ghostly father, I me confess,
    First to God and then to you,
    That at a window – wot ye how? –
I stole a kiss of great sweetness,
Which done was out avisedness;
    But it is done not undone now.
My ghostly father, I me confess,
    First to God and then to you.
But I restore it shall doubtless
    Again, if so be that I mow;
    And that to God I make a vow
And else I ask forgiveness.
My ghostly father, I me confess,
    First to God and then to you.

ST TERESA OF AVILA

O my supreme God! O my Rest! The graces that You had granted me till then should have been enough, seeing that Your compassion and greatness had brought me along so many devious ways to so secure a state, and to a house where there were so many servants of God from whom I might have learnt how to advance in Your service. When I remember the manner of my profession, the great resolution and joy with which I made it, and my betrothal to You, I do not know how to go on. I cannot speak of this without tears. Indeed they should be of blood and my heart should break, and that would be a slight repentance for all the offences I have committed against You since then. It seems to me now that I had good reason for not desiring this great honour, since I was to make very poor use of it. But You, my Lord, were prepared for me to misuse Your grace for almost twenty years, and to accept the injury so that I might become better. It seems, O God, as if I had promised to break all the promises I had made You, though this was not my intention at the time. When I look back on these actions of mine I do not know what my intentions were. But what they clearly reveal, O my Spouse, is the difference between You and myself. My joy at having been the means whereby the multitude of Your mercies has been made known certainly

19

moderates my sorrow for my great sins. In whom, Lord, can those mercies shine out as they do in me, who thus obscured the great graces that You began to work in me by my evil deeds? Alas, O my Creator, if I try to offer an excuse, I have none. No one is to blame but I. If I had repaid You any of the love that You were beginning to show me, I could have since bestowed it on no one but You, and with that all would have been made well. But since I did not deserve it, and had no such good fortune, may Your mercy avail me now, O Lord!

ANDREW MARVELL

'To His Coy Mistress'

Had we but world enough, and time,
This coyness, Lady, were no crime.
We would sit down and think which way
To walk and pass our long love's day.
Thou by the Indian Ganges' side
Shouldst rubies find: I by the tide
Of Humber would complain. I would
Love you ten years before the Flood,
And you should, if you please, refuse
Till the conversion of the Jews.
My vegetable love should grow
Vaster than empires, and more slow;
An hundred years should go to praise
Thine eyes and on thy forehead gaze;
Two hundred to adore each breast;
But thirty thousand to the rest;
An age at least to every part,
And the last age should show your heart;
For, Lady, you deserve this state,
Nor would I love at lower rate.
    But at my back I always hear

Time's wingèd chariot hurrying near;
And yonder all before us lie
Deserts of vast eternity.
Thy beauty shall no more be found,
Nor, in thy marble vault, shall sound
My echoing song: then worms shall try
That long preserved virginity,
And your quaint honour turn to dust,
And into ashes all my lust:
The grave's a fine and private place,
But none, I think, do there embrace.

   Now therefore, while the youthful hue
Sits on thy skin like morning dew,
And while thy willing soul transpires
At every pore with instant fires,
Now let us sport us while we may,
And now, like amorous birds of prey,
Rather at once our time devour
Than languish in his slow-chapt power.
Let us roll all our strength and all
Our sweetness up into one ball,
And tear our pleasures with rough strife
Thorough the iron gates of life:
Thus, though we cannot make our sun
Stand still, yet we will make him run.

CHARLES DICKENS

from *David Copperfield*

We went into the house, which was cheerfully lighted up, and into a hall where there were all sorts of hats, caps, great-coats, plaids, gloves, whips, and walking-sticks. 'Where is Miss Dora?' said Mr Spenlow to the servant. 'Dora!' I thought. 'What a beautiful name!'

We turned into a room near at hand (I think it was the identical breakfast-room, made memorable by the brown East Indian sherry), and I heard a voice say, 'Mr Copperfield, my daughter Dora, and my daughter Dora's confidential friend!' It was, no doubt, Mr Spenlow's voice, but I didn't know it, and I didn't care whose it was. All was over in a moment. I had fulfilled my destiny. I was a captive and a slave. I loved Dora Spenlow to distraction!

She was more than human to me. She was a Fairy, a Sylph, I don't know what she was – anything that no one ever saw, and everything that everybody ever wanted. I was swallowed up in an abyss of love in an instant. There was no pausing on the brink; no looking down, or looking back; I was gone, head-long, before I had sense to say a word to her.

'I,' observed a well-remembered voice, when I had

bowed and murmured something, 'have seen Mr Copperfield before.'

The speaker was not Dora. No; the confidential friend, Miss Murdstone!

I don't think I was much astonished. To the best of my judgment, no capacity of astonishment was left in me. There was nothing worth mentioning in the material world, but Dora Spenlow, to be astonished about. I said, 'How do you do, Miss Murdstone? I hope you are well.' She answered, 'Very well.' I said, 'How is Mr Murdstone?' She replied, 'My brother is robust, I am obliged to you.'

Mr Spenlow, who, I suppose, had been surprised to see us recognise each other, then put in his word.

'I am glad to find,' he said, 'Copperfield, that you and Miss Murdstone are already acquainted.'

'Mr Copperfield and myself,' said Miss Murdstone, with severe composure, 'are connexions. We were once slightly acquainted. It was in his childish days. Circumstances have separated us since. I should not have known him.'

I replied that I should have known her, anywhere. Which was true enough.

'Miss Murdstone has had the goodness,' said Mr Spenlow to me, 'to accept the office – if I may so describe it – of my daughter Dora's confidential friend. My daughter Dora having, unhappily, no mother, Miss Murdstone is obliging enough to become her companion and protector.'

A passing thought occurred to me that Miss Murdstone, like the pocket instrument called a life-preserver, was not so much designed for purposes of protection as of assault. But as I had none but passing thoughts for any subject save Dora, I glanced at her, directly afterwards, and was thinking that I saw, in her prettily pettish manner, that she was not very much inclined to be particularly confidential to her companion and protector, when a bell rang, which Mr Spenlow said was the first dinner-bell, and so carried me off to dress.

The idea of dressing one's self, or doing anything in the way of action, in that state of love, was a little too ridiculous. I could only sit down before my fire, biting the key of my carpet-bag and think of the captivating, girlish, bright-eyed, lovely Dora. What a form she had, what a face she had, what a graceful, variable, enchanting manner!

The bell rang again so soon that I made a mere scramble of my dressing, instead of the careful operation I could have wished under the circumstances, and went down-stairs. There was some company. Dora was talking to an old gentleman with a grey head. Grey as he was – and a great-grandfather into the bargain, for he said so – I was madly jealous of him.

What a state of mind I was in! I was jealous of everybody. I couldn't bear the idea of anybody knowing Mr Spenlow better than I did. It was torturing to me to hear them talk of occurrences in which I had had no share. When a most amiable person, with a highly polished bald head, asked me across the dinner-table, if that were the first occasion of my seeing the grounds, I could have done anything to him that was savage and revengeful.

I don't remember who was there, except Dora. I have not the least idea what we had for dinner, besides Dora. My impression is, that I dined off Dora entirely, and sent away half-a-dozen plates untouched. I sat next to her. I talked to her. She had the most delightful little voice, the gayest little laugh, the pleasantest and most fascinating little ways, that ever led a lost youth into hopeless slavery. She was rather diminutive altogether. So much the more precious, I thought.

When she went out of the room with Miss Murdstone (no other ladies were of the party), I fell into a reverie, only disturbed by the cruel apprehension that Miss Murdstone would disparage me to her. The amiable creature with the polished head told me a long story, which I think was about gardening. I think I heard him say, 'my gardener', several times. I seemed to pay the deepest attention to him, but I was wandering in a garden of Eden all the while, with Dora.

JOHN O'KEEFE

'Amo, Amas'

Amo, Amas, I love a lass
As a cedar tall and slender;
Sweet cowslip's grace is her nominative case,
And she's of the feminine gender.

    Rorum, Corum, sunt divorum,
    Harum, Scarum divo;
    Tag-rag, merry-derry, periwig and hat-band
    Hic hoc horum genitivo.

Can I decline a Nymph divine?
Her voice as a flute is dulcis.
Her oculus bright, her manus white,
And soft, when I tacto, her pulse is.

    Rorum, Corum, sunt divorum,
    Harum, Scarum divo;
    Tag-rag, merry-derry, periwig and hat-band
    Hic-hoc horum genitivo.

Oh, how bella my puella,
I'll kiss secula seculorum.
If I've luck, sir, she's my uxor,
O dies benedictorum.

Rorum, Corum, sunt divorum,
Harum, Scarum divo;
Tag-rag, merry-derry, periwig and hat-band
Hic hoc horum genitivo.

IVAN TURGENEV

from *On the Eve*

'Well, good-bye, Dmitri Nikanorich,' she began; 'but as we have met now, at least give me your hand in parting.'

Insarov was on the point of holding out his hand. 'No, I can't even do that,' he muttered, and turned away again.

'You can't?'

'I can't. Good-bye.' And he turned to the door of the chapel.

'Wait another moment,' said Elena. 'You seem to be afraid of me. But I'm braver than you are,' she added, feeling herself shiver slightly all over. 'I can tell you . . . do you want me to tell you? . . . why you found me here? Do you know where I was going?'

Insarov looked at her in surprise.

'I was coming to you.'

'To me?'

Elena covered her face with her hands. 'You wanted to make me say that I love you,' she whispered. 'Well, I've said it.'

'Elena!' cried Insarov.

She took her hands away, looked at him, and fell on his breast. He held her in his arms – and remained silent. He did

29

not need to tell her that he loved her. By the tone of his exclamation, by the sudden transformation of his whole being, by the rise and fall of his breast which she clung to so confidently, by the way he touched her hair with his fingers, Elena could not but feel that he loved her. He was silent – and she had no need of words. 'He is here, he loves me . . . what more can I want?' The stillness of rapture, the stillness of an unyielding anchor, of an end accomplished; the supreme stillness that gives beauty and meaning even to death, endued her with its divine potency. She wanted nothing because she had everything.

'Oh, my brother, my friend, my love!' her lips whispered, and she could not tell if it was her heart or his that throbbed so blissfully and meltingly in her breast.

He stood motionless; his strong arms held in a close embrace the young life that had surrendered itself to him; and he felt against his breast a new and infinitely precious burden. A feeling of beatitude, of ineffable thankfulness, shook the strong roots of his heart, and for the first time in his life tears welled up in his eyes.

But she, she did not cry; she only repeated, 'Oh, my friend, my brother.'

'So you'll come with me wherever I go?' he asked her a quarter of an hour later, still holding her and supporting her in his arms.

'Wherever you go – to the end of the world. Where you are, I'll be there too.'

'And you aren't deluding yourself? You know that your parents will never agree to our marriage?'

'I'm not deluding myself, I know it.'

'You know that I'm poor, almost a beggar?'

'I do.'

'That I'm not Russian, that it isn't my destiny to live in

Russia, that you'll have to sever all your ties with your country, your people?'

'I do, I do.'

'You know, too, that I've dedicated myself to a hard, unrewarding task, that I, that we, may have to face not only dangers but poverty and humiliation?'

'Yes, I know it all . . . I love you.'

'That you will have to give up all the things you are used to, that alone out there among strangers you may have to work . . . ?'

She put her hand over his mouth. 'I love you, my dearest one.'

He began to kiss the slender, rosy fingers passionately. Elena did not pull away her hand from his lips and, with childish delight, and laughing curiosity, watched him cover her hand and her fingers with his kisses. Suddenly she flushed and hid her face against his breast. He raised her head tenderly and looked deeply into her eyes.

'Welcome then,' he said to her, 'my wife before man and before God!'

OVID

♥

Elegy 5

In summer's heat and mid-time of the day
To rest my limbs upon a bed I lay,
One window shut, the other open stood,
Which gave such light, as twinkles in a wood,
Like twilight glimpse at setting of the sun,
Or night being past, and yet not day begun.
Such light to shamefast maidens must be shown,
Where they must sport, and seem to be unknown.
Then came Corinna in a long loose gown,
Her white neck hid with tresses hanging down:
Resembling fair Semiramis going to bed
Or Layis of a thousand wooers sped.
I snatched her gown, being thin, the harm was small,
Yet strived she to be covered there withal.
And striving thus as one that would be cast,
Betrayed herself, and yielded at the last.
Stark naked as she stood before mine eye,
Not one wen in her body could I spy.
What arms and shoulders did I touch and see,
How apt her breasts were to be pressed by me.
How smooth a belly under her waist saw I?

How large a leg, and what a lusty thigh?
To leave the rest, all liked me passing well,
I clinged her naked body, down she fell,
Judge you the rest, being tired she bade me kiss,
Jove send me more such afternoons as this.

translated by
Christopher Marlowe

JOHN WILMOT, EARL OF ROCHESTER

'A Song of a Young Lady to Her Ancient Lover'

Ancient person, for whom I
All the flattering youth defy,
Long be it ere thou grow old,
Aching, shaking, crazy, cold;
    But still continue as thou art,
    Ancient person of my heart.

On thy withered lips and dry,
Which like barren furrows lie,
Brooding kisses I will pour
Shall thy youthful heat restore
(Such kind showers in autumn fall,
And a second spring recall);
    Nor from thee will ever part,
    Ancient person of my heart.

Thy nobler part, which but to name
In our sex would be counted shame,
By age's frozen grasp possessed,
From his ice shall be released,
And soothed by my reviving hand,

In former warmth and vigor stand.
All a lover's wish can reach
For thy joy my love shall teach,
And for thy pleasure shall improve
All that art can add to love.
    Yet still I love thee without art,
    Ancient person of my heart.

GEOFFREY CHAUCER

from 'Merciless Beauty'

Your eyen two will slay me suddenly;
I may the beauty of them not sustain,
So woundeth it throughout my hearte keen.

And but your word will healen hastily
My hearte's wounde, while that it is green,
   Your eyen two will slay me suddenly;
   I may the beauty of them not sustain.

Upon my trŭth I say you faithfully
That ye bin of my life and death the queen;
For with my death the truthe shall be seen.
   Your eyen two will slay me suddenly;
   I may the beauty of them not sustain,
   So woundeth it throughout my hearte keen.

SIR PHILIP SIDNEY

from the Countess of Pembroke's *Arcadia*

My true love hath my heart, and I have his,
By just exchange one for the other given.
I hold his dear, and mine he cannot miss:
There never was a better bargain driven.
His heart in me keeps me and him in one;
My heart in him his thoughts and senses guides;
He loves my heart, for once it was his own;
I cherish his, because in me it bides.
His heart his wound received from my sight;
My heart was wounded with his wounded heart;
For as from me on him his hurt did light,
So still, methought, in me his hurt did smart;
   Both equal hurt, in this change sought our bliss:
   My true love hath my heart, and I have his.

ANONYMOUS

'Donal Og'

It is late last night the dog was speaking of you;
the snipe was speaking of you in her deep marsh.
It is you are the lonely bird through the woods;
and that you may be without a mate until you find me.

You promised me, and you said a lie to me,
that you would be before me where the sheep are flocked;
I gave a whistle and three hundred cries to you,
and I found nothing there but a bleating lamb.

You promised me a thing that was hard for you,
a ship of gold under a silver mast;
twelve towns with a market in all of them,
and a fine white court by the side of the sea.

You promised me a thing that is not possible,
that you would give me gloves of the skin of a fish;
that you would give me shoes of the skin of a bird;
and a suit of the dearest silk in Ireland.

When I go by myself to the Well of Loneliness,
I sit down and I go through my trouble;
when I see the world and do not see my boy,
he that has an amber shade in his hair.

It was on that Sunday I gave my love to you;
the Sunday that is last before Easter Sunday.
And myself on my knees reading the Passion;
and my two eyes giving love to you for ever.

My mother said to me not to be talking with you today,
or tomorrow, or on the Sunday;
it was a bad time she took for telling me that;
it was shutting the door after the house was robbed.

My heart is as black as the blackness of the sloe,
or as the black coal that is on the smith's forge;
or as the sole of a shoe left in white halls;
it was you put that darkness over my life.

You have taken the east from me; you have taken the west
    from me;
you have taken what is before me and what is behind me;
you have taken the moon, you have taken the sun from me;
and my fear is great that you have taken God from me!

EMILY BRONTË

from *Wuthering Heights*

With straining eagerness Catherine gazed towards the
entrance of her chamber. He did not hit the right room
directly; she motioned me to admit him; but he found it out,
ere I could reach the door, and in a stride or two was at her
side, and had her grasped in his arms.

He neither spoke nor loosed his hold for some five
minutes, during which period he bestowed more kisses than
ever he gave in his life before, I dare say: but then my
mistress had kissed him first, and I plainly saw that he could
hardly bear, for downright agony, to look into her face! The
same conviction had stricken him as me, from the instant
he beheld her, that there was no prospect of ultimate
recovery there – she was fated, sure to die.

'Oh, Cathy! Oh, my life! how can I bear it?' was the first
sentence he uttered, in a tone that did not seek to disguise
his despair. And now he stared at her so earnestly that I
thought the very intensity of his gaze would bring tears into
his eyes; but they burned with anguish: they did not melt.

'What now?' said Catherine, leaning back, and returning
his look with a suddenly clouded brow: her humour was a
mere vane for constantly varying caprices. 'You and Edgar

have broken my heart, Heathcliff! And you both come to bewail the deed to me, as if you were the people to be pitied! I shall not pity you, not I. You have killed me – and thriven on it, I think. How strong you are! How many years do you mean to live after I am gone?'

Heathcliff had knelt on one knee to embrace her; he attempted to rise, but she seized his hair, and kept him down.

'I wish I could hold you,' she continued, bitterly, 'till we were both dead! I shouldn't care what you suffered. I care nothing for your sufferings. Why shouldn't you suffer? I do! Will you forget me? Will you be happy when I am in the earth? Will you say twenty years hence, "That's the grave of Catherine Earnshaw. I loved her long ago, and was wretched to lose her; but it is past. I've loved many others since: my children are dearer to me than she was; and, at death, I shall not rejoice that I am going to her: I shall be sorry that I must leave them!" Will you say so, Heathcliff?'

'Don't torture me till I'm as mad as yourself,' cried he, wrenching his head free, and grinding his teeth.

The two, to a cool spectator, made a strange and fearful picture. Well might Catherine deem that heaven would be a land of exile to her, unless with her mortal body she cast away her mortal character also. Her present countenance had a wild vindictiveness in its white cheek, and a bloodless lip and scintillating eye; and she retained in her closed fingers a portion of the locks she had been grasping. As to her companion, while raising himself with one hand, he had taken her arm with the other; and so inadequate was his stock of gentleness to the requirements of her condition, that on his letting go I saw four distinct impressions left blue in the colourless skin.

'Are you possessed with a devil,' he pursued, savagely, 'to talk in that manner to me when you are dying? Do you reflect that all those words will be branded in my memory, and eating deeper eternally after you have left me? You know you lie to say I have killed you: and, Catherine, you know that I could as soon forget you as my existence! Is it not sufficient for your infernal selfishness, that while you are at peace I shall writhe in the torments of hell?'

'I shall not be at peace,' moaned Catherine, recalled to a sense of physical weakness by the violent, unequal throbbing of her heart, which beat visibly and audibly under this excess of agitation. She said nothing further till the paroxysm was over; then she continued, more kindly –

'I'm not wishing you greater torment than I have, Heathcliff. I only wish us never to be parted: and should a word of mine distress you hereafter, think I feel the same distress underground, and for my own sake, forgive me! Come here and kneel down again! You never harmed me in your life. Nay, if you nurse anger, that will be worse to remember than my harsh words! Won't you come here again? Do!'

Heathcliff went to the back of her chair, and leant over, but not so far as to let her see his face, which was livid with emotion. She bent round to look at him; he would not permit it: turning abruptly, he walked to the fire-place, where he stood, silent, with his back towards us. Mrs Linton's glance followed him suspiciously: every movement woke a new sentiment in her. After a pause, and a prolonged gaze, she resumed; addressing me in accents of indignant disappointment –

'Oh, you see, Nelly, he would not relent a moment to keep me out of the grave. *That* is how I'm loved! Well, never mind. That is not *my* Heathcliff. I shall love mine yet; and take him

42

with me: he's in my soul. And,' added she musingly, 'the thing that irks me most is this shattered prison, after all. I'm tired, tired of being enclosed here. I'm wearying to escape into that glorious world, and to be always there: not seeing it dimly through tears, and yearning for it through the walls of an aching heart; but really with it, and in it. Nelly, you think you are better and more fortunate than I; in full health and strength: you are sorry for me – very soon that will be altered. I shall be sorry for *you*. I shall be incomparably beyond and above you all. I *wonder* he won't be near me!' She went on to herself. 'I thought he wished it. Heathcliff, dear! you should not be sullen now. Do come to me, Heathcliff.'

In her eagerness she rose and supported herself on the arm of the chair. At that earnest appeal he turned to her, looking absolutely desperate. His eyes wide, and wet at last, flashed fiercely on her; his breast heaved convulsively. An instant they held asunder, and then how they met I hardly saw, but Catherine made a spring, and he caught her, and they were locked in an embrace from which I thought my mistress would never be released alive: in fact, to my eyes, she seemed directly insensible. He flung himself into the nearest seat, and on my approaching hurriedly to ascertain if she had fainted, he gnashed at me, and foamed like a mad dog, and gathered her to him with greedy jealousy. I did not feel as if I were in the company of a creature of my own species: it appeared that he would not understand, though I spoke to him; so I stood off, and held my tongue, in great perplexity.

A movement of Catherine's relieved me a little presently: she put up her hand to clasp his neck, and bring her cheek to his as he held her; while he, in return, covering her with frantic caresses, said wildly –

'You teach me now how cruel you've been – cruel and false. *Why* did you despise me? *Why* did you betray your own heart, Cathy? I have not one word of comfort. You deserve this. You have killed yourself. Yes, you may kiss me, and cry; and wring out my kisses and tears: they'll blight you – they'll damn you. You loved me – then what *right* had you to leave me? What right – answer me – for the poor fancy you felt for Linton? Because misery, and degradation, and death, and nothing that God or Satan could inflict would have parted us, *you*, of your own will, did it. I have not broken your heart – *you* have broken it; and in breaking it, you have broken mine. So much the worse for me, that I am strong. Do I want to live? What kind of living will it be when you – oh, God! would *you* like to live with your soul in the grave?'

'Let me alone. Let me alone,' sobbed Catherine. 'If I've done wrong, I'm dying for it. It is enough! You left me too: but I won't upbraid you! I forgive you. Forgive me!'

'It is hard to forgive, and to look at those eyes, and feel those wasted hands,' he answered. 'Kiss me again; and don't let me see your eyes! I forgive what you have done to me. I love *my* murderer – but *yours*! How can I?'

They were silent – their faces hid against each other, and washed by each other's tears. At least, I suppose the weeping was on both sides; as it seemed Heathcliff *could* weep on a great occasion like this.

EDMUND WALLER

Song

   Go, lovely rose –
Tell her that wastes her time and me,
   That now she knows,
When I resemble her to thee,
How sweet and fair she seems to be.

   Tell her that's young,
And shuns to have her graces spied,
   That hadst thou sprung
In deserts where no men abide,
Thou must have uncommended died.

   Small is the worth
Of beauty from the light retired:
   Bid her come forth,
Suffer herself to be desired,
And not blush so to be admired.

   Then die! – that she
The common fate of all things rare

May read in thee;
How small a part of time they share
That are so wondrous sweet and fair!

ROBERT BURNS

'A Red, Red Rose'

O my Luve's like a red, red rose,
    That's newly sprung in June;
O my Luve's like the melodie
    That's sweetly play'd in tune. –

As fair art thou, my bonnie lass,
    So deep in luve am I;
And I will love thee still, my Dear,
    Till a' the seas gang dry. –

Till a' the seas gang dry, my Dear,
    And the rocks melt wi' the sun:
I will love thee still, my Dear,
    While the sands o' life shall run. –

And fare thee weel, my only Luve!
    And fare thee weel, a while!
And I will come again, my Luve,
    Tho' it were ten thousand mile!

FRANÇOIS VILLON

'The Old Lady's Lament for Her Youth'

I think I heard the belle
we called the Armouress
lamenting her lost youth;
this was her whore's language:
'Oh treacherous, fierce old age,
you've gnawed me with your tooth,
yet if I end this mess
and die, I go to hell.

'You've stolen the great power
my beauty had on squire,
clerk, monk and general;
once there was no man born
who wouldn't give up all
(whatever his desire)
to have me for an hour –
this body beggars scorn!

'Once I broke the crown's laws,
and fled priests with a curse,
because I kept a boy,
and taught him what I knew –
alas, I only threw

myself away, because
I wanted to enjoy
this pimp, who loved my purse.

'I loved him when he hid
money, or used to bring
home whores and smash my teeth –
Oh when I lay beneath,
I forgave everything –
my tongue stuck to his tongue!
Tell me what good I did?
What's left? Disease and dung.

'He's dead these thirty years,
and I live on, grow old,
and think of that good time,
what was, what I've become;
sometimes, when I behold
my naked flesh, so numb,
dry, poor and small with time,
I cannot stop my tears.

'Where's my large Norman brow,
arched lashes, yellow hair,
the wide-eyed looks I used
to trap the cleverest men?
Where is my clear, soft skin,
neither too brown or fair,
my pointed ears, my bruised
red lips? I want to know.

'Where's the long neck I bent
swanlike, when asking pardon?
My small breasts, and the lips
of my vagina that sat
inside a little garden

and overlooked my hips,
plump, firm and so well set
for love's great tournament?

'Now wrinkled cheeks, and thin
wild lashes; nets of red
string fill the eyes that used
to look and laugh men dead.
How nature has abused
me. Wrinkles plough across
the brow, the lips are skin,
my ears hang down like moss.

'This is how beauty dies:
humped shoulders, barrenness
of mind; I've lost my hips,
vagina, and my lips.
My breasts? They're a retreat!
Short breath – how I repeat
my silly list! My thighs
are blotched like sausages.

'This is how we discuss
ourselves, and nurse desire
here as we gab about
the past, boneless as wool
dolls by a greenwood fire –
soon lit, and soon put out.
Once I was beautiful . . .
That's how it goes with us.'

translated by
Robert Lowell

ANONYMOUS

I gently touched her hand: she gave
A look that did my soul enslave;
I pressed her rebel lips in vain:
They rose up to be pressed again.
    Thus happy, I no farther meant,
    Than to be pleased and innocent.

On her soft breasts my hand I laid,
And a quick, light impression made;
They with a kindly warmth did glow,
And swelled, and seemed to overflow.
    Yet, trust me, I no farther meant,
    Than to be pleased and innocent.

On her eyes my eyes did stay:
O'er her smooth limbs my hands did stray;
Each sense was ravished with delight,
And my soul stood prepared for flight.
    Blame me not if at last I meant
    More to be pleased than innocent.

THOMAS CAMPION

'I Care Not for These Ladies'

I care not for these ladies
That must be wooed and prayed:
Give me kind Amaryllis,
The wanton country maid.
Nature Art disdaineth;
Her beauty is her own.
   Who when we court and kiss,
   She cries; 'Forsooth, let go!'
   But when we come where comfort is,
   She never will say no.

If I love Amaryllis,
She gives me fruit and flowers;
But if we love these ladies,
We must give golden showers.
Give them gold that sell love,
Give me the nut-brown lass,
   Who when we court and kiss,
   She cries: 'Forsooth, let go!'
   But when we come where comfort is,
   She never will say no.

These ladies must have pillows
And beds by strangers wrought.
Give me a bower of willows
Of moss and leaves unbought,
And fresh Amaryllis
With milk and honey fed,
    Who when we court and kiss,
    She cries: 'Forsooth, let go!'
    But when we come where comfort is,
    She never will say no.

♥

'The Ballad of Andrew Lammie'

At the Mill o Tifty's lived a man
In the neighbourhood o Fyvie:
For he had a lovely daughter fair
An they ca'ed her bonny Annie.

Her bloom was like the springin flower
That hails the rosy mornin,
And her innocence and graceful mien
Her beauteous face adornin.

Noo her hair was fair and her eyes were blue
And her cheeks as red as roses,
And her countenance was fair tae view
And they ca'ed her bonny Annie.

Noo Lord Fyvie had a trumpeter
Wha's name was Andra Lammie,
And he had the airt for tae gain the hairt
O the Mill of Tifty's Annie.

Noo her mother cried her tae the door,
Sayin, 'Come here to me, my Annie.
Did e'er ye see a prettier man
Than the trumpeter o Fyvie?'

Oh but naethin she said, but sighin sair,
'Twas alas for bonny Annie!
For she durstnae own that her hairt was won
By the trumpeter o Fyvie.

And at nicht when all went tae their bed,
A'slept fu' soond but Annie;
Love so oppressed her tender breast,
And love will waste her body.

Oh love comes in to my bedside,
And love will lie beyond me;
Love so oppressed my tender breast,
And love will waste my body.

'My love I go tae Edinburgh toon,
An for a while maun leave thee.'
'Oh but I'll be deid afore ye come back
In the green kirk yaird o Fyvie.'

So her father struck her wondrous sore
An also did her mother,
And her sisters also took their score,
But woe be tae her brother!

Her brother struck her wondrous sore
Wi cruel strokes and many,
And he broke her back owre the temple-stane,
Aye the temple-stane o Fyvie.

'Oh mother dear please make my bed,
And lay my face tae Fyvie,
For I will lie and I will die
For my dear Andra Lammie.'

Noo when Andra hame frae Edinburgh came
Wi muckle grief and sorrow:
'My love she died for me last night,
So I'll die for her tomorrow.'

MATTHEW PRIOR

'A True Maid'

'No, no; for my virginity,
  'When I lose that,' says Rose, 'I'll die':
'Behind the elms last night,' cried Dick,
  'Rose, were you not extremely sick?'

WILLIAM SHAKESPEARE

♥

from *Romeo and Juliet*

ROMEO He jests at scars that never felt a wound.
           [*Enter* JULIET *above.*]
But soft, what light through yonder window breaks?
It is the east and Juliet is the sun!
Arise fair sun and kill the envious moon
Who is already sick and pale with grief
That thou her maid art far more fair than she.
Be not her maid since she is envious,
Her vestal livery is but sick and green
And none but fools do wear it. Cast it off.
It is my lady, O it is my love!
O that she knew she were!
She speaks, yet she says nothing. What of that?
Her eye discourses, I will answer it.
I am too bold. 'Tis not to me she speaks.
Two of the fairest stars in all the heaven,
Having some business, do entreat her eyes.
To twinkle in their spheres till they return.
What if her eyes were there, they in her head?
The brightness of her cheek would shame those stars
As daylight doth a lamp. Her eyes in heaven

Would through the airy region stream so bright
That birds would sing and think it were not night.
See how she leans her cheek upon her hand.
O that I were a glove upon that hand,
That I might touch that cheek.

JULIET Ay me.

ROMEO She speaks.
O speak again bright angel, for thou art
As glorious to this night, being o'er my head,
As is a winged messenger of heaven
Unto the white-upturned wondering eyes
Of mortals that fall back to gaze on him
When he bestrides the lazy-puffing clouds
And sails upon the bosom of the air.

JULIET O Romeo, Romeo, wherefore art thou Romeo?
Deny thy father and refuse thy name.
Or if thou wilt not, be but sworn my love
And I'll no longer be a Capulet.

ROMEO Shall I hear more, or shall I speak at this?

JULIET 'Tis but thy name that is my enemy:
Thou art thyself, though not a Montague.
What's Montague? It is nor hand nor foot
Nor arm nor face nor any other part
Belonging to a man. O be some other name.
What's in a name? That which we call a rose
By any other word would smell as sweet;
So Romeo would, were he not Romeo call'd,
Retain that dear perfection which he owes
Without that title. Romeo, doff thy name,
And for thy name, which is no part of thee,
Take all myself.

ROMEO I take thee at thy word.
Call me but love, and I'll be new baptis'd:

Henceforth I never will be Romeo.

JULIET What man art thou that thus bescreen'd in night
So stumblest on my counsel?

ROMEO By a name
I know not how to tell thee who I am:
My name, dear saint, is hateful to myself
Because it is an enemy to thee.
Had I it written, I would tear the word.

JULIET My ears have yet not drunk a hundred words
Of thy tongue's uttering, yet I know the sound.
Art thou not Romeo, and a Montague?

ROMEO Neither, fair maid, if either thee dislike.

JULIET How cam'st thou hither, tell me, and wherefore?
The orchard walls are high and hard to climb,
And the place death, considering who thou art,
If any of my kinsmen find thee here.

ROMEO With love's light wings did I o'erperch these walls,
For stony limits cannot hold love out,
And what love can do, that dares love attempt:
Therefore thy kinsmen are no stop to me.

JULIET If they do see thee, they will murder thee.

ROMEO Alack, there lies more peril in thine eye
Than twenty of their swords. Look thou but sweet
And I am proof against their enmity.

JULIET I would not for the world they saw thee here.

ROMEO I have night's cloak to hide me from their eyes,
And but thou love me, let them find me here.
My life were better ended by their hate
Than death prorogued, wanting of thy love.

JULIET By whose direction found'st thou out this place?

ROMEO By love, that first did prompt me to enquire.
He lent me counsel, and I lent him eyes.
I am no pilot, yet wert thou as far

As that vast shore wash'd with the farthest sea,
I should adventure for such merchandise.

JULIET Thou knowest the mask of night is on my face,
Else would a maiden blush bepaint my cheek
For that which thou hast heard me speak tonight.
Fain would I dwell on form; fain, fain deny
What I have spoke. But farewell, compliment.
Dost thou love me? I know thou wilt say 'Ay',
And I will take thy word. Yet, if thou swear'st,
Thou mayst prove false. At lovers' perjuries,
They say, Jove laughs. O gentle Romeo,
If thou dost love, pronounce it faithfully.
Or, if thou think'st I am too quickly won,
I'll frown and be perverse and say thee nay,
So thou wilt woo; but else, not for the world.
In truth, fair Montague, I am too fond,
And therefore thou mayst think my haviour light,
But trust me, gentleman, I'll prove more true
Than those that have more cunning to be strange.
I should have been more strange, I must confess,
But that thou overheard'st, ere I was ware,
My true-love passion; therefore pardon me,
And not impute this yielding to light love
Which the dark night hath so discovered.

ROMEO Lady, by yonder blessed moon I vow,
That tips with silver all these fruit-tree tops——

JULIET O swear not by the moon, th'inconstant moon,
That monthly changes in her circled orb,
Lest that thy love prove likewise variable.

ROMEO What shall I swear by?

JULIET Do not swear at all.
Or if thou wilt, swear by thy gracious self,
Which is the god of my idolatry,

61

And I'll believe thee.

ROMEO If my heart's dear love——

JULIET Well, do not swear. Although I joy in thee,
I have no joy of this contract tonight:
It is too rash, too unadvis'd, too sudden,
Too like the lightning, which doth cease to be
Ere one can say 'It lightens'. Sweet, good night.
This bud of love, by summer's ripening breath,
May prove a beauteous flower when next we meet.
Good night, good night. As sweet repose and rest
Come to thy heart as that within my breast.

ROMEO O wilt thou leave me so unsatisfied?

JULIET What satisfaction canst thou have tonight?

ROMEO Th'exchange of thy love's faithful vow for mine.

JULIET I gave thee mine before thou didst request it,
And yet I would it were to give again.

ROMEO Wouldst thou withdraw it? For what purpose, love?

JULIET But to be frank and give it thee again;
And yet I wish but for the thing I have.
My bounty is as boundless as the sea,
My love as deep: the more I give to thee
The more I have, for both are infinite.
I hear some noise within. Dear love, adieu.

[Nurse *calls within.*]

Anon, good Nurse – Sweet Montague be true.
Stay but a little, I will come again.   [*Exit* Juliet.]

ROMEO O blessed blessed night. I am afeard,
Being in night, all this is but a dream,
Too flattering sweet to be substantial.

[*Enter* Juliet *above.*]

JULIET Three words, dear Romeo, and good night indeed.
If that thy bent of love be honourable,

Thy purpose marriage, send me word tomorrow
By one that I'll procure to come to thee,
Where and what time thou wilt perform the rite,
And all my fortunes at thy foot I'll lay,
And follow thee my lord throughout the world.

NURSE [*Within.*] Madam.

JULIET I come, anon – But if thou meanest not well I do
beseech thee——

NURSE [*Within.*] Madam.

JULIET By and by I come——
To cease thy strife and leave me to my grief.

THOMAS HARDY

'A Thunderstorm in Town'

She wore a new 'terra-cotta' dress,
And we stayed, because of the pelting storm,
Within the hansom's dry recess,
Though the horse had stopped: yea, motionless
  We sat on, snug and warm.

Then the downpour ceased, to my sharp sad pain
And the glass that had screened our forms before
Flew up, and out she sprang to her door:
I should have kissed her if the rain
  Had lasted a minute more.

HECTOR BERLIOZ

from *Memoirs*

My old apartment in the rue Richelieu where I lived before going to Rome had, I discovered, been let. Some impulse moved me to take rooms in the house opposite, 1 rue Neuve-Saint-Marc, which Miss Smithson had at one time occupied. Next day, meeting the old servant who had for many years been housekeeper to the establishment, I asked what had become of Miss Smithson and whether she had heard any news of her. 'But sir, didn't you . . . She's in Paris, she was staying here only a few days ago. She left the day before yesterday and moved to the rue de Rivoli. She was in the apartment that you have now. She is director of an English company that's opening next week.' I stood aghast at the extraordinary series of coincidences. It was fate. I saw it was no longer possible for me to struggle against it. For two years I had heard nothing of the fair Ophelia; I had had no idea where she was, whether in England, Scotland or America; and here I was, arriving from Italy at exactly the moment when she reappeared after a tour of northern Europe. We had just missed meeting each other in the same house; I had taken the apartment that she had left the previous evening.

A believer in the magnetic attractions and secret affinities of the heart would find in all this some fine arguments to support his theories. Without going so far, I reasoned as follows: I had come to Paris to have my new work (the monodrama) performed. If I went to the English theatre and saw her again before I had given my concert, the old delirium tremens would inevitably seize me. As before, I would lose all independence of will and be incapable of the attention and concentrated effort which the enterprise demanded. Let me first give my concert. Afterwards I would see her, whether as Ophelia or as Juliet, even if it killed me; I would give myself up to the destiny which seemed to pursue me, and not struggle any more.

Therefore, though the dread Shakespearean names beckoned to me daily from the walls of Paris, I resisted their blandishments and the concert was arranged.

The programme consisted of my Fantastic Symphony followed by its sequel *Lélio* or *The Return to Life*, the monodrama which forms the second part of the 'Episode in the Life of an Artist'. The subject of this musical drama, as is known, was none other than my love for Miss Smithson and the anguish and 'bad dreams' it had brought me. Now consider the incredible chain of accidents which follows.

Two days before the concert – which I thought of as a farewell to art and life – I was in Schlesinger's music shop when an Englishman came in and almost immediately went out again. 'Who was that?' I asked Schlesinger, moved by a curiosity for which there was no rational motive. 'That's Schutter, who writes for *Galignani's Messenger*. Wait a moment,' he added, striking his forehead, 'I have an idea. Let me have a box for your concert. Schutter knows Miss Smithson. I'll ask him to take her the tickets and persuade her to come.' The suggestion made me shudder, but I lacked the strength of mind to reject it. I gave him the tickets. Schlesinger ran after Schutter, caught him up, and doubtless explained what a stir the presence of the famous actress would create. Schutter promised to do everything he could to get her there.

While I was occupied with rehearsals and all the other preparations, the unfortunate director of the English company was busy ruining herself. The guileless actress had been counting on the continued enthusiasm of the Parisians and on the support of the new school of writers who three years earlier had lauded both Shakespeare and his interpreter to the skies. But Shakespeare was no longer a novelty to the feckless and frivolous public. The literary revolution demanded by the romantics had been achieved; and not only were the leaders of the movement not eager for any further demonstration of the power of the greatest of all dramatic poets: unconsciously, they feared it. It was not in their interests that the public should become too familiar with works from which they had borrowed so extensively.

The result was that the English company excited little response, and receipts were low. It had been an expensive venture. The season showed a deficit which absorbed the imprudent director's entire capital. This was the situation when Schutter called on Miss Smithson and offered her a box for my concert, and this is what ensued. She herself told me long afterwards.

Schutter found her in a state of profound despondency, and his proposal was at first badly received. At such a moment it was hardly to be expected she should have time for music. But Miss Smithson's sister joined with him in urging her to accept: it would be a distraction for her; and an English actor, who was with them, on his side appeared anxious to take advantage of the offer. A cab was summoned, and Miss Smithson allowed herself, half willingly, half forcibly, to be escorted into it. The triumphant Schutter gave the address: 'The Conservatoire,' and they were off. On the way the unhappy creature glanced at the programme. My name had not been mentioned. She now learnt that I was the originator of the proceedings. The title of the symphony and the headings of the various movements somewhat astonished her; but it never so much as occurred to her that the heroine of this strange and doleful drama might be herself.

On entering the stage box above a sea of musicians (for I had collected a very large orchestra), she was aware of a buzz of interest all over the hall. Everyone seemed to be staring in her direction; a thrill of emotion went through her, half excitement, half fear, which she could not clearly account for. Habeneck was conducting. When I came in and sat breathlessly down behind him, Miss Smithson, who until then had supposed she might have mistaken the name at the head of the programme, recognised me. 'Yes, it is he,' she murmured; 'poor young man, I expect he has forgotten me; at least . . . I hope he has.' The symphony began and produced a tremendous effect. (Those were days when the hall of the Conservatoire, from which I am now excluded, was the focus of immense public enthusiasm.) The brilliant reception, the passionate character of the work, its ardent, exalted melodies, its protestations of love, its sudden outbursts of violence, and the sensation of hearing an orchestra of that size close to, could not fail to make an impression – an impression as profound as it was totally unexpected – on her nervous system and poetic imagination, and in her heart of hearts she thought, 'Ah, if he still loved me!' During the interval which followed the performance of the symphony, the ambiguous remarks of Schutter, and of Schlesinger too – for he had been unable to resist coming into her box – and their veiled allusions to the cause of this young composer's well-known troubles of the heart, began to make her suspect the truth, and she heard them in growing agitation. But when Bocage, the actor who spoke the part of Lélio (that is, myself), declaimed these lines:

> Oh, if I could only find her, the Juliet, the Ophelia whom my heart cries out for! If I could drink deep of the mingled joy and sadness that real love offers us, and one autumn evening on some wild heath with the north wind blowing over it, lie in her arms and sleep a last, long, sorrowful sleep!

'God!' she thought: 'Juliet – Ophelia! Am I dreaming? I can no longer doubt. It is of me he speaks. He loves me still.' From that moment, so she has often told me, she felt the room reel about her; she heard no more but sat in a dream, and at the end returned home like a sleepwalker, with no clear notion of what was happening.

The date was 9 December 1832.

CHRISTOPHER MARLOWE

from 'Hero and Leander'

Thence flew love's arrow with the golden head,
And thus Leander was enamoured.
Stone-still he stood, and evermore he gazed,
Till with the fire that from his countenance blazed
Relenting Hero's gentle heart was strook;
Such force and virtue hath an amorous look.
   It lies not in our power to love or hate,
For will in us is over-ruled by fate.
When two are stripped, long ere the course begin,
We wish that one should lose, the other win;
And one especially do we affect
Of two gold ingots, like in each respect.
The reason no man knows; let it suffice,
What we behold is censured by our eyes.
Where both deliberate, the love is slight;
Who ever loved, that loved not at first sight?
   He kneeled, but unto her devoutly prayed;
Chaste Hero to herself thus softly said:
'Were I the saint he worships, I would hear him';
And as she spake these words, came somewhat near him.
He started up; she blushed as one ashamed;

Wherewith Leander much more was inflamed.
He touched her hand; in touching it she trembled;
Love deeply grounded hardly is dissembled.
These lovers parlied by the touch of hands;
True love is mute, and oft amazed stands.
Thus while dumb signs their yielding hearts entangled,
The air with sparks of living fire was spangled,
And night, deep drenched in misty Acheron,
Heaved up her head, and half the world upon
Breathed darkness forth (dark night is Cupid's day).
And now begins Leander to display
Love's holy fire with words, with sighs and tears,
Which like sweet music entered Hero's ears.

JOHN KEATS

❧

Letters to Fanny Brawne

February (?) 1820

My dear Fanny,

    Do not let your mother suppose that you hurt me by writing at night. For some reason or other your last night's note was not so treasureable as former ones. I would fain that you call me *Love* still. To see you happy and in high spirits is a great consolation to me – still let me believe that you are not half so happy as my restoration would make you. I am nervous, I own, and may think myself worse than I really am; if so you must indulge me, and pamper with that sort of tenderness you have manifested towards me in different Letters. My sweet creature when I look back upon the pains and torments I have suffer'd for you from the day I left you to go to the Isle of Wight; the ecstasies in which I have pass'd some days and the miseries in their turn, I wonder the more at the Beauty which has kept up the spell so fervently. When I send this round I shall be in the front parlour watching to see you show yourself for a minute in the garden. How illness stands as a barrier betwixt me and you! Even if I was well – I must make myself as good a Philosopher as possible. Now I have had opportunities of passing nights anxious and awake I have found other thoughts intrude upon me. 'If I should die,' said I to myself, 'I have left no immortal work behind me – nothing to make my friends proud of my memory – but I have lov'd the principle of beauty in all things, and if I had had time I would have made myself remember'd.' Thoughts like these came very feebly whilst I was in health and every pulse beat for you – now you divide with this (may *I* say it?) 'last infirmity of noble minds' all my reflection.

God bless you, Love.

J Keats.

February (?) 1820

My dearest Fanny,

Then all we have to do is to be patient. Whatever violence I may sometimes do myself by hinting at what would appear to any one but ourselves a matter of necessity, I do not think I could bear any approach of a thought of losing you. I slept well last night, but cannot say that I improve very fast. I shall expect you tomorrow, for it is certainly better that I should see you seldom. Let me have your good night. Your affectionate

J——K——

February (?) 1820

My dearest Girl, how could it ever have been my wish to forget you? how could I have said such a thing? The utmost stretch my mind has been capable of was to endeavour to forget you for your own sake seeing what a chance there was of my remaining in a precarious state of health. I would have borne it as I would bear death if fate was in that humour: but I should as soon think of choosing to die as to part from you. Believe too my Love that our friends think

73

and speak for the best, and if their best is not our best it is not their fault, When I am better I will speak with you at large on these subjects, if there is any occasion – I think there is none. I am rather nervous today perhaps from being a little recovered and suffering my mind to take little excursions beyond the doors and windows. I take it for a good sign, but as it must not be encouraged you had better delay seeing me till tomorrow. Do not take the trouble of writing much: merely send me my good night. Remember me to your Mother and Margaret. Your affectionate

J——K——

ALEXANDER PUSHKIN

from *Eugene Onegin*

Tatyana's letter, treasured ever
as sacred, lies before me still.
I read with secret pain, and never
can read enough to get my fill.
Who taught her an address so tender,
such careless language of surrender?
Who taught her all this mad, slapdash,
heartfelt, imploring, touching trash
fraught with enticement and disaster?
It baffles me. But I'll repeat
here a weak version, incomplete,
pale transcript of a vivid master
or *Freischütz* as it might be played
by nervous hands of a schoolmaid:

Tatyana's Letter to Onegin

'I write to you – no more confession
is needed, nothing's left to tell.
I know it's now in your discretion
with scorn to make my world a hell.

But, if you've kept some faint impression
of pity for my wretched state,
you'll never leave me to my fate.
At first I thought it out of season
to speak; believe me: of my shame
you'd not so much as know the name,
if I'd possessed the slightest reason
to hope that even once a week
I might have seen you, heard you speak
on visits to us, and in greeting
I might have said a word, and then
thought, day and night, and thought again
about one thing, till our next meeting.
But you're not sociable, they say:
you find the country godforsaken;
though we . . . don't shine in any way,
our joy in you is warmly taken.

'Why did you visit us, but why?
Lost in our backwoods habitation
I'd not have known you, therefore I
would have been spared this laceration.
In time, who knows, the agitation
of inexperience would have passed,
I would have found a friend, another,
and in the role of virtuous mother
and faithful wife I'd have been cast.

'Another! . . . No, another never
in all the world could take my heart!
Decreed in highest court for ever . . .
heaven's will – for you I'm set apart;
and my whole life has been directed

and pledged to you, and firmly planned;
I know, Godsent one, I'm protected
until the grave by your strong hand:
you'd made appearance in my dreaming;
unseen, already you were dear,
my soul had heard your voice ring clear,
stirred at your gaze, so strange, so gleaming,
long, long ago . . . no, that could be
no dream. You'd scarce arrived, I reckoned
to know you, swooned, and in a second
all in a blaze, I said: it's he!

'You know, it's true, how I attended,
drank in your words when all was still –
helping the poor, or while I mended
with balm of prayer my torn and rended
spirit that anguish had made ill.
At this midnight of my condition,
was it not you, dear apparition,
who in the dark came flashing through
and, on my bed-head gently leaning,
with love and comfort in your meaning,
spoke words of hope? But who are you:
the guardian angel of tradition,
or some vile agent of perdition
sent to seduce? Resolve my doubt.
Oh, this could all be false and vain,
a sham that trustful souls work out;
fate could be something else again . . .

'So let it be! for you to keep
I trust my fate to your direction,
henceforth in front of you I weep,

77

I weep, and pray for your protection . . .
Imagine it: quite on my own
I've no one here who comprehends me,
and now a swooning mind attends me,
dumb I must perish, and alone.
My heart awaits you: you can turn it
to life and hope with just a glance –
or else disturb my mournful trance
with censure – I've done all to earn it!

'I close. I dread to read this page . . .
for shame and fear my wits are sliding . . .
and yet your honour is my gage,
and in it boldly I'm confiding . . .'

Now Tanya's groaning, now she's sighing;
the letter trembles in her grip;
the rosy sealing-wafer's drying
upon her feverish tongue; the slip
from off her charming shoulder's drooping,
and sideways her poor head is stooping.
But now the radiance of the moon
is dimmed. Down there the valley soon
comes clearer through the mists of dawning.
Down there, by slow degrees, the stream
has taken on a silvery gleam;
the herdsman's horn proclaimed the morning
and roused the village long ago:
to Tanya, all's an empty show.

BEN JONSON

'To Celia'

Drink to me only with thine eyes,
    And I will pledge with mine;
Or leave a kiss but in the cup
    And I'll not look for wine.
The thirst that from the soul doth rise
    Doth ask a drink divine;
But might I of Jove's nectar sup,
    I would not change for thine.

I sent thee late a rosy wreath,
    Not so much honouring thee
As giving it a hope that there
    It could not withered be;
But thou thereon didst only breathe,
    And sent'st it back to me;
Since when it grows, and smells, I swear,
    Not of itself but thee!

RIHAKU

'The River-merchant's Wife: A Letter'

While my hair was still cut straight across my forehead
I played about the front gate, pulling flowers.
You came by on bamboo stilts, playing horse,
You walked about my seat, playing with blue plums.
And we went on living in the village of Chokan:
Two small people, without dislike or suspicion.

At fourteen I married My Lord you.
I never laughed, being bashful.
Lowering my head, I looked at the wall.
Called to, a thousand times, I never looked back.

At fifteen I stopped scowling,
I desired my dust to be mingled with yours
For ever and for ever and for ever.
Why should I climb the look out?

At sixteen you departed,
You went into far Ku-to-yen, by the river of swirling
   eddies,
And you have been gone five months.
The monkeys make sorrowful noise overhead.

You dragged your feet when you went out.
By the gate now, the moss is grown, the different mosses,
Too deep to clear them away!
The leaves fall early this autumn, in wind.
The paired butterflies are already yellow with August
Over the grass in the West garden;
They hurt me. I grow older.
If you are coming down through the narrows of the river
    Kiang,
Please let me know beforehand,
And I will come out to meet you
                    As far as Cho-fu-Sa.

translated by
Ezra Pound

GILES FLETCHER

'Wooing Song'

Love is the blossom where there blows
Every thing that lives or grows:
Love doth make the Heav'ns to move,
And the Sun doth burn in love:
Love the strong and weak doth yoke,
And makes the ivy climb the oak,
Under whose shadows lions wild,
Soften'd by love, grow tame and mild:
Love no med'cine can appease,
He burns the fishes in the seas:
Not all the skill his wounds can stench,
Not all the sea his fire can quench.
Love did make the bloody spear
Once a leavy coat to wear,
While in his leaves there shrouded lay
Sweet birds, for love that sing and play
And of all love's joyful flame
I the bud and blossom am.
    Only bend thy knee to me,
    Thy wooing shall thy winning be!

See, see the flowers that below
Now as fresh as morning blow;
And of all the virgin rose
That as bright Aurora shows;
How they all unleavèd die,
Losing their virginity!
Like unto a summer shade,
But now born, and now they fade.
Every thing doth pass away;
There is danger in delay:
Come, come, gather then the rose,
Gather it, or it you lose!
All the sand of Tagus' shore
Into my bosom casts his ore:
All the valleys' swimming corn
To my house is yearly borne:
Every grape of every vine
Is gladly bruised to make me wine:
While ten thousand kings, as proud,
To carry up my train have bow'd,
And a world of ladies send me
In my chambers to attend me:
All the stars in Heav'n that shine,
And ten thousand more, are mine:
   Only bend thy knee to me,
   Thy wooing shall thy winning be!

ROBERT HERRICK

'Upon Julia's Clothes'

When as in silks my Julia goes,
Then, then (me thinks) how sweetly flows
The liquefaction of her clothes.

Next, when I cast mine eyes and see
That brave vibration each way free,
O how that glittering taketh me!

STEVIE SMITH

'Barlow'

I'm growing much fonder of Barlow
And I think of him a lot
And sometimes I think I'm in love with him
And wish I was not.

For Barlow's my sister's fancy
The son of the Bishop of Bye
And if he should plump for the younger
That's me, the elder would die.

Oh I see by each curve and each wrinkle
Of each delicate lid of each eye
If Barlow should plump for the younger
The elder would certainly die.

SERGEI AKSAKOV

❧

from *A Russian Schoolboy*

There happened about this time at Kazan a remarkable incident in which I was directly concerned. A private school for boys and girls was kept in the town by a German couple of the name of Wilfing. Having no children of their own, they had adopted a destitute orphan, Marya Kermik, who was now grown up and very pretty. Kartashevsky sometimes called on the Wilfings and took me there twice; but, at the time I am speaking of, I had not been there for more than six months. A chance meeting in the course of a jaunt out of the town renewed the acquaintance; and the girl's beauty soon asserted its influence over me. I naturally revealed my secret to my bosom friend, Panaev; he was delighted, embraced me warmly, and congratulated me on 'beginning to live'. He used every effort to fan the spark which had dropped upon my youthful heart. As Marya was a very quiet modest girl, all her many admirers sighed for her at a respectful distance; and of my feelings she had of course no idea. Visionary hopes and visionary disappointments, which I expressed in wretched boyish verses, were still going on when suddenly a mysterious traveller, a Swedish Count, turned up at Kazan for a short stay. He made the acquaintance of the Wilfings and charmed them all; he went there daily and spent the whole day at their house. He was a handsome man of about thirty-five, clever, pleasant, and lively, a skilful artist and a master of many languages, and an author as well both in verse and prose. In three days, the Wilfings were raving about him; in a week Marya had fallen in love with him; and, at the end of another fortnight, he married her and carried her off with him to Siberia, where he had been sent by Government to conduct some scientific investigation, with an official to act as interpreter, because the Count himself did not understand a word of Russian. The Wilfings found it hard to part with their adopted daughter whom they loved as if she had been their own; but they did not venture to complain of a match which seemed so enviable, so astonishing, and so dazzling. She was a baker's daughter, and she had married a Count, who adored his wife and was richly endowed with every gift of nature and education. People less simple than the Wilfings might easily have been seduced by an event so wonderful.

But alas! the riddle was soon explained. The Count had conferred this title on himself; he was a notorious swindler and adventurer, well known for his exploits in Germany under the name of Aschenbrenner. From Germany he had fled to Russia for fear of the police; he became a Russian subject and spent several years in the western provinces, where he was implicated in many frauds and finally banished to Siberia. The official who accompanied him was a police officer with a German name, whose business it was to convey his charge incognito to Irkutsk, and hand him over personally to the governor there for rigorous supervision. But all these facts were somehow kept from the public and from the Wilfings.

The traveller had no need of an interpreter; for it was afterwards discovered that he spoke Russian very well. In the course of his journey he himself wrote to the Wilfings and informed them of the imposture; he said he had been driven to it by the irresistible power of love; of course he called himself the victim of calumny, and hoped to be cleared and compensated for his undeserved sufferings. His wife wrote too: she said that, though she knew all, she still thanked God for her happiness. Later, someone sent to the Wilfings a German work in two volumes, which contained a narrative of the sham Count's adventures written by himself. The man was the Vidocq of his time. The old Wilfings were inconsolable. I never could find out what was Marya's ultimate fate. Such was the sorrowful ending of my first love-story.

CHARLES DICKENS

❧

from *Great Expectations*

Miss Havisham beckoned her to come close, and took up a jewel from the table, and tried its effect upon her fair young bosom and against her pretty brown hair. 'Your own, one day, my dear, and you will use it well. Let me see you play cards with this boy.'

'With this boy! Why, he is a common labouring-boy!'

I thought I overheard Miss Havisham answer – only it seemed so unlikely – 'Well? You can break his heart.'

'What do you play, boy?' asked Estella of myself, with the greatest disdain.

'Nothing but beggar my neighbour, Miss.'

'Beggar him,' said Miss Havisham to Estella. So we sat down to cards.

It was then I began to understand that everything in the room had stopped, like the watch and the clock, a long time ago. I noticed that Miss Havisham put down the jewel exactly on the spot from which she had taken it up. As Estella dealt the cards, I glanced at the dressing-table again, and saw that the shoe upon it, once white, now yellow, had never been worn. I glanced down at the foot from which the shoe was absent, and saw that the silk stocking on it, once white, now yellow, had been trodden ragged. Without this arrest of everything, this standing still of all the pale decayed objects, not even the withered bridal dress on the collapsed form could have looked so like grave-clothes, or the long veil so like a shroud.

So she sat, corpse-like, as we played at cards; the frillings and trimmings on her bridal dress, looking like earthy paper. I knew nothing then of the discoveries that are occasionally made of bodies buried in ancient times, which fall to powder in the moment of being distinctly seen; but, I have often thought since, that she must have looked as if the admission of the natural light of day would have struck her to dust.

'He calls the knaves, Jacks, this boy!' said Estella with disdain, before our first game was out. 'And what coarse hands he has! And what thick boots!'

I had never thought of being ashamed of my hands before; but I began to consider them a very indifferent pair. Her contempt for me was so strong, that it became infectious, and I caught it.

She won the game, and I dealt. I misdealt, as was only natural, when I knew she was lying in wait for me to do wrong; and she denounced me for a stupid, clumsy labouring-boy.

'You say nothing of her,' remarked Miss Havisham to me, as she looked on.' She says many hard things of you, yet you say nothing of her. What do you think of her?'

'I don't like to say,' I stammered.

'Tell me in my ear,' said Miss Havisham, bending down.

'I think she is very proud,' I replied, in a whisper.

'Anything else?'

'I think she is very pretty.'

'Anything else?'

'I think she is very insulting.' (She was looking at me then with a look of supreme aversion.)

'Anything else?'

'I think I should like to go home.'

'And never see her again, though she is so pretty?'

'I am not sure that I shouldn't like to see her again, but I should like to go home now.'

'You shall go soon,' said Miss Havisham aloud. 'Play the game out.'

Saving for the one weird smile at first, I should have felt almost sure that Miss Havisham's face could not smile. It had dropped into a watchful and brooding expression – most likely when all the things about her had become transfixed – and it looked as if nothing could ever lift it up again. Her chest had dropped, so that she stooped, and her voice had dropped, so that she spoke low, and with a dead lull upon her; altogether, she had the appearance of having dropped, body and soul, within and without, under the weight of a crushing blow.

I played the game to an end with Estella, and she beggared me. She threw the cards down on the table when she had won them all, as if she despised them for having been won of me.

'When shall I have you here again?' said Miss Havisham. 'Let me think.'

I was beginning to remind her that today was Wednesday, when she checked me with her former impatient movement of the fingers of her right hand.

'There! there! I know nothing of days of the week; I know nothing of weeks of the year. Come again after six days. You hear?'

'Yes, ma'am.'

'Estella, take him down. Let him have something to eat,

and let him roam and look about him while he eats. Go, Pip.'

I followed the candle down, as I had followed the candle up, and she stood it in the place where we had found it. Until she opened the side entrance, I had fancied, without thinking about it, that it must necessarily be night-time. The rush of the daylight quite confounded me, and made me feel as if I had been in the candlelight of the strange room many hours.

'You are to wait here, you boy,' said Estella; and disappeared and closed the door.

I took the opportunity of being alone in the court-yard, to look at my coarse hands and my common boots. My opinion of those accessories was not favourable. They had never troubled me before, but they troubled me now, as vulgar appendages. I determined to ask Joe why he had ever taught me to call those picture-cards, Jacks, which ought to be called knaves. I wished Joe had been rather more genteelly brought up, and then I should have been so too.

She came back, with some bread and meat and a little mug of beer. She put the mug down on the stones of the yard, and gave me the bread and meat without looking at me, as insolently as if I were a dog in disgrace. I was so humiliated, hurt, spurned, offended, angry, sorry – I cannot hit upon the right name for the smart – God knows what its name was – that tears started to my eyes. The moment they sprang there, the girl looked at me with a quick delight in having been the cause of them. This gave me power to keep them back and to look at her: so, she gave a contemptuous toss – but with a sense, I thought, of having made too sure that I was so wounded – and left me.

But, when she was gone, I looked about me for a place to hide my face in, and got behind one of the gates in the brewery-lane, and leaned my sleeve against the wall there, and leaned my forehead on it and cried. As I cried, I kicked the wall, and took a hard twist at my hair; so bitter were my feelings, and so sharp was the smart without a name, that needed counteraction.

LOUIS MacNEICE

from 'Trilogy for X'

And love hung still as crystal over the bed
   And filled the corners of the enormous room;
The boom of dawn that left her sleeping, showing
   The flowers mirrored in the mahogany table.

O my love, if only I were able
   To protract this hour of quiet after passion,
Not ration happiness but keep this door for ever
   Closed on the world, its own world closed within it.

But dawn's waves trouble with the bubbling minute,
   The names of books come clear upon their shelves,
The reason delves for duty and you will wake
   With a start and go on living on your own.

The first train passes and the windows groan,
   Voices will hector and your voice become
A drum in tune with theirs, which all last night
   Like sap that fingered through a hungry tree
Asserted our one night's identity.

JANE AUSTEN

from *Persuasion*

. . . and sinking into the chair which he had occupied, succeeding to the very spot where he had leaned and written, her eyes devoured the following words:

I can listen no longer in silence. I must speak to you by such means as are within my reach. You pierce my soul. I am half agony, half hope. Tell me not that I am too late, that such precious feelings are gone for ever. I offer myself to you again with a heart even more your own than when you almost broke it, eight years and a half ago. Dare not say that man forgets sooner than woman, that his love has an earlier death. I have loved none but you. Unjust I may have been, weak and resentful I have been, but never inconstant. You alone have brought me to Bath. For you alone, I think and plan. Have you not seen this? Can you fail to have understood my wishes? I had not waited even these ten days, could I have read your feelings, as I think you must have penetrated mine. I can hardly write. I am every instant hearing something which over-powers me. You sink your voice, but I can distinguish the tones of that voice when they would be lost on others. Too good, too excellent creature! You do us justice, indeed. You do believe that there is true attachment and constancy among men. Believe it to be most fervent, most undeviating, in

F. W.

I must go, uncertain of my fate; but I shall return hither or follow your party, as soon as possible. A word, a look, will be enough to decide whether I enter your father's house this evening or never.

Such a letter was not soon to be recovered from. Half an hour's solitude and reflexion might have tranquillised her; but the ten minutes only which now passed before she was interrupted, with all the restraints of her situation, could do nothing towards tranquillity. Every moment rather brought fresh agitation. It was an overpowering happiness.

ELIZABETH BARRETT BROWNING

Sonnet 43, from the Portuguese

How do I love thee? Let me count the ways.
I love thee to the depth and breadth and height
My soul can reach, when feeling out of sight
For the ends of Being and ideal Grace
I love thee to the level of every day's
Most quiet need, by sun and candlelight.
I love thee freely, as men strive for Right;
I love thee purely, as they turn from Praise.
I love thee with the passion put to use
In my old griefs, and with my childhood's faith.
I love thee with a love I seemed to lose
With my lost saints, – I love thee with the breath,
Smiles, tears, of all my life! – and, if God choose,
I shall but love thee better after death.

MARK TWAIN

♥

from *The Adventures of Tom Sawyer*

When school broke up at noon, Tom flew to Becky
Thatcher, and whispered in her ear:

'Put on your bonnet and let on you're going home; and
when you get to the corner, give the rest of 'em the slip, and
turn down through the lane and come back. I'll go the other
way and come it over 'em the same way.'

So the one went off with one group of scholars, and the
other with another. In a little while the two met at the
bottom of the lane, and when they reached the school they
had it all to themselves. Then they sat together, with a slate
before them, and Tom gave Becky the pencil and held her
hand in his, guiding it, and so created another surprising
house. When the interest in art began to wane, the two fell
to talking. Tom was swimming in bliss. He said:

'Do you love rats?'

'No! I hate them!'

'Well, I do too – *live* ones. But I mean dead ones; to swing
round your head with a string.'

'No, I don't care for rats much, anyway. What *I* like, is
chewing-gum.'

'O, I should say so! I wish I had some now.'

'Do you? I've got some. I'll let you chew it a while, but you must give it back to me.'

That was agreeable, so they chewed it turn about, and dangled their legs against the bench in excess of contentment.

'Was you ever at a circus?' said Tom.

'Yes, and my pa's going to take me again some time, if I'm good.'

'I been to the circus three or four times – lots of times. Church ain't shucks to a circus. There's things going on at a circus all the time. I'm going to be a clown in a circus when I grow up.'

'O, are you? That will be nice. They're so lovely, all spotted up.'

'Yes, that's so. And they get slathers of money – most a dollar a day, Ben Rogers says. Say, Becky, was you ever engaged?'

'What's that?'

'Why, engaged to be married.'

'No.'

'Would you like to?'

'I reckon so. I don't know. What is it like?'

'Like? Why it ain't like anything. You only just tell a boy you won't ever have anybody but him, ever .ever *ever*, and then you kiss and that's all. Anybody can do it.'

'Kiss? What do you kiss for?'

'Why that, you know, is to – well, they always do that.'

'Everybody?'

'Why yes, everybody that's in love with each other. Do you remember what I wrote on the slate?'

'Ye-yes.'

'What was it?'

'I shan't tell you.'

'Shall I tell *you*?'

'Ye-yes – but some other time.'

'No, now.'

'No, not now – tomorrow.'

'O, no, *now*. Please, Becky – I'll whisper it. I'll whisper it ever so easy.'

Becky hesitating, Tom took silence for consent, and passed his arm about her waist and whispered the tale ever so softly, with his mouth close to her ear. And then he added:

'Now you whisper it to me – just the same.'

She resisted, for a while, and then said:

'You turn your face away so you can't see, and then I will. But you mustn't ever tell anybody – *will* you, Tom? Now you won't, *will* you?'

'No, indeed indeed I won't. Now, Becky.'

He turned his face away. She bent timidly around till her breath stirred his curls and whispered, 'I – love – you!'

Then she sprang away and ran around and around the desks and benches, with Tom after her, and took refuge in a corner at last, with her little white apron to her face. Tom clasped her about her neck and pleaded:

'Now Becky, it's all done – all over but the kiss. Don't you be afraid of that – it ain't anything at all. Please, Becky.' And he tugged at the apron and the hands.

By and by she gave up, and let her hands drop; her face, all glowing with the struggle, came up and submitted. Tom kissed the red lips and said:

'Now it's all done, Becky. And always after this, you know, you ain't ever to love anybody but me, and you ain't ever to marry anybody but me, never never and forever. Will you?'

'No, I'll never love anybody but you, Tom, and I'll never

marry anybody but you – and you ain't to ever marry anybody but me, either.'

'Certainly. Of course. That's *part* of it. And always coming to school or when we're going home, you're to walk with me, when there ain't anybody looking – and you choose me and I choose you at parties, because that's the way you do when you're engaged.'

'It's so nice. I never heard of it before.'

'Oh it's ever so gay! Why me and Amy Lawrence——'

The big eyes told Tom his blunder and he stopped, confused.

'O, Tom! Then I ain't the first you've ever been engaged to!'

The child began to cry. Tom said:

'O don't cry, Becky. I don't care for her any more.'

'Yes you do, Tom – you know you do.'

Tom tried to put his arm about her neck, but she pushed him away and turned her face to the wall, and went on crying. Tom tried again, with soothing words in his mouth, and was repulsed again. Then his pride was up, and he strode away and went outside. He stood about, restless and uneasy, for a while, glancing at the door, every now and then, hoping she would repent and come to find him. But she did not. Then he began to feel badly and fear that he was in the wrong. It was a hard struggle with him to make new advances, now, but he nerved himself to it and entered. She was still standing back there in the corner, sobbing, with her face to the wall. Tom's heart smote him. He went to her and stood a moment, not knowing exactly how to proceed. Then he said hesitatingly:

'Becky, I – I don't care for anybody but you.'

No reply – but sobs.

'Becky,' – pleadingly. 'Becky, won't you say something?'

More sobs.

Tom got out his chiefest jewel, a brass knob from the top of an andiron, and passed it around her so that she could see it, and said:

'Please, Becky, won't you take it?'

She struck it to the floor. Then Tom marched out of the house and over the hills and far away, to return to school no more that day. Presently Becky began to suspect. She ran to the door; he was not in sight; she flew around to the play-yard; he was not there. Then she called:

'Tom! Come back, Tom!'

She listened intently, but there was no answer. She had no companions but silence and loneliness. So she sat down to cry again and upbraid herself; and by this time the scholars began to gather again, and she had to hide her griefs and still her broken heart and take up the cross of a long, dreary, aching afternoon, with none among the strangers about her to exchange sorrows with.

ANONYMOUS

'I Saw My Lady Weep'

I saw my lady weep
And Sorrow proud to be advanced so
In those fair eyes where all perfections keep.
   Her face was full of woe;
But such a woe, believe me, as wins more hearts
Than Mirth can do with her enticing parts.

   Sorrow was there made fair,
And Passion wise, tears a delightful thing;
Silence beyond all speech a wisdom rare.
   She made her sighs to sing,
And all things with so sweet a sadness move
As made my heart at once both grieve and love.

   O fairer than aught else
The world can show, leave off in time to grieve.
Enough, enough your joyful looks excels;
   Tears kills the heart, believe.
   O strive not to be excellent in woe,
Which only breeds your beauty's overthrow.

LEO TOLSTOY

♦

from *Anna Karenina*

Vronsky did not even try to sleep that night. He sat in his place, his eyes staring straight before him, not observing the people who went in or out; and if previously his appearance of imperturbable calm had struck and annoyed those who did not know him, he now seemed to them even prouder and more self-confident. He looked at people as if they were inanimate things. A nervous young man, a Law Court official, who sat opposite, hated him for that look. The young man repeatedly lit his cigarette at Vronsky's, talked to him, and even jostled him to prove that he was not a thing but a man; yet Vronsky still looked at him as at a street lamp, and the young man made grimaces, feeling that he was losing self-control under the stress of this refusal to regard him as human.

Vronsky neither saw nor heard anyone. He felt himself a king, not because he believed that he had made an impression on Anna – he did not yet believe that – but because the impression she had made on him filled him with happiness and pride.

What would come of it all he did not know and did not even consider. He felt that all his powers, hitherto dissipated and scattered, were now concentrated and directed with terrible energy toward one blissful aim. This made him happy. He knew only that he had told her the truth: that he would go where she went, that all the happiness of life and the only meaning of life for him now was in seeing and hearing her. When he had got out of the train at Bologoe station to drink a glass of seltzer water and had seen Anna, he had involuntarily at once told her just what he was thinking about. He was glad he had said it to her, and that she now knew it and was thinking about it. He did not sleep at all that night. When he returned to the train, he kept recalling all the positions in which he had seen her, and all her words; and in his imagination, causing his heart to stand still, floated pictures of a possible future.

When he got out of the train at Petersburg he felt, despite his sleepless night, as fresh and animated as after a cold bath. He stopped outside the carriage, waiting till she appeared. 'I shall see her again,' he thought and smiled involuntarily. 'I shall see her walk, her face . . . she will say something, turn her head, look at me, perhaps even smile.' But before seeing her he saw her husband, whom the station-master was respectfully conducting through the crowd. 'Dear me! the husband!' Only now did Vronsky for the first time clearly realise that the husband was connected with her. He knew she had a husband, but had not believed in his existence, and only fully believed in him when he saw him there: his head and shoulders, and the black trousers containing his legs, and especially when he saw that husband with an air of ownership quietly take her hand.

When he saw Karenin, with his fresh Petersburg face, his sternly self-confident figure, his round hat and his slightly rounded back, Vronsky believed in his existence, and had such a disagreeable sensation as a man tortured by thirst might feel on reaching a spring and finding a dog, sheep, or pig in it, drinking the water and making it muddy. Karenin's gait, the swinging of his thighs, and his wide short feet, particularly offended Vronsky, who acknowledged only his own unquestionable right to love Anna. But she was still the same, and the sight of her still affected him physically, exhilarating and stimulating him and filling him with joy. He ordered his German valet, who had run up from a second-class carriage, to get his luggage and take it home, and he himself went up to her. He saw the husband and wife meet, and with the penetration of a lover he noticed the signs of slight embarrassment when she spoke to her husband.

'No, she doesn't and can't love him,' he decided mentally.

While he was approaching her from behind he observed with joy that she became aware of his approach and was about to turn but, on recognising him, again addressed her husband.

'Did you have a good night?' he inquired, bowing toward them both, and leaving it to Karenin to take the greeting as meant for himself and to recognise him, or not, as he pleased.

'Yes, quite comfortable, thank you,' she replied.

Her face seemed tired and had none of that play which showed now in a smile and now in the animation of her eyes; but just for an instant as she looked at him he saw a gleam in her eyes and, though the spark was at once extinguished, that one instant made him happy. She glanced at her husband to see whether he knew Vronsky. Karenin looked at him with displeasure, absently trying to recall who he might be. Vronsky's calm self-confidence struck like a scythe on a stone against the cold self-confidence of Karenin.

'Count Vronsky,' said Anna.

'Ah! I believe we have met before,' said Karenin, extending his hand with indifference. 'You travelled there with the mother and came back with the son,' he said, uttering every word distinctly as though it were something valuable he was giving away. 'I suppose you are returning from furlough?' he remarked; and without waiting for an answer said to his wife in his playful manner: 'Well, were many tears shed in Moscow over the parting?'

By addressing himself thus to his wife he conveyed to Vronsky his wish to be alone with her, and turning to Vronsky he touched his hat. But Vronsky, addressing Anna, said:

'I hope to have the honour of calling on you.'

Karenin glanced at him with his weary eyes.

'I shall be very pleased,' he said coldly. 'We are at home on Mondays.' Then having finally dismissed Vronsky he said to his wife in his usual bantering tone: 'What a good thing it was that I had just half an hour to spare to meet you and was able to show my devotion!'

'You insist too much on your devotion, for me to value it greatly,' she replied in the same playful tone, while she involuntarily listened to the sound of Vronsky's footsteps following them. 'But what does he matter to me?' she asked herself, and began inquiring of her husabnd how Serezha had got on during her absence.

MATTHEW PRIOR

'A Better Answer to Cloe Jealous'

Dear Cloe, how blubbered is that pretty face,
  Thy cheek all on fire, and thy hair all uncurled:
Pr'ythee quit this caprice; and (as old Falstaff says)
  Let us e'en talk a little like folks of this world.

How canst thou presume thou hast leave to destroy
  The beauties, which Venus but lent to thy keeping?
Those looks were designed to inspire love and joy:
  More ord'nary eyes may serve people for weeping.

To be vexed at a trifle or two that I writ,
  Your judgment at once and my passion you wrong:
You take that for fact, which will scarce be found wit:
  Od's life! must one swear to the truth of a song?

What I speak, my fair Cloe, and what I write, shows
  The diff'rence there is betwixt nature and art:
I court others in verse, but I love thee in prose:
  And they have my whimsies, but thou hast my heart.

The god of us verse-men (you know, child) the sun,
    How after his journeys he sets up his rest:
If at morning o'er earth 'tis his fancy to run,
    At night he reclines on his Thetis's breast.

So when I am wearied with wand'ring all day,
    To thee, my delight, in the evening I come:
No matter what beauties I saw in my way;
    They were but my visits, but thou art my home.

Then finish, dear Cloe, this pastoral war;
    And let us, like Horace and Lydia, agree:
For thou art a girl as much brighter than her,
    As he was a poet sublimer than me.

ROBERT GREENE

'A Night Visitor'

Cupid abroad was lated in the night;
   His wings were wet with ranging in the rain.
Harbour he sought; to me he took his flight:
   To dry his plumes I heard the boy complain,
      I oped the door and granted his desire;
      I rose myself, and made the wag a fire.

Looking more narrow by the fire's flame,
   I spied his quiver hanging by his back.
Doubting the boy might my misfortune frame,
   I would have gone for fear of further wrack.
      But what I drad, did me poor wretch betide:
      For forth he drew an arrow from his side.

He pierced the quick, and I began to start,
   A pleasing wound but that it was too high;
His shaft procured a sharp yet sugared smart.
   Away he flew, for why his wings were dry,
      But left the arrow sticking in my breast,
      That sore I grieved I welcomed such a guest.

SIR PHILIP SIDNEY

from 'Astrophil and Stella'

On Cupid's bow how are my heart-strings bent,
    That see my wrack, and yet embrace the same!
    When most I glory, then I feel most shame:
I willing run, yet while I run, repent.
My best wits still their own disgrace invent;
    My very ink turns straight to Stella's name;
    And yet my words, as them my pen doth frame,
Avise themselves that they are vainly spent.
    For though she pass all things, yet what is all
That unto me, who fare like him that both
Looks to the skies, and in a ditch doth fall?
O let me prop my mind, yet in his growth,
    And not in nature for best fruits unfit.
    'Scholar,' saith Love, 'bend hitherward your wit.'

WALT WHITMAN

'When I Heard at the Close of the Day'

When I heard at the close of the day how my name had been
   receiv'd with plaudits in the capitol, still it was not a
   happy night for me that follow'd,
And else when I carous'd, or when my plans were
   accomplish'd, still I was not happy,
But the day when I rose at dawn from the bed of perfect
   health, refresh'd, singing, inhaling the ripe breath of
   autumn,
When I saw the full moon in the west grow pale and
   disappear in the morning light,
When I wander'd alone over the beach, and undressing
   bathed, laughing with the cool waters, and saw the sun
   rise,
And when I thought how my dear friend my lover was on
   his way coming, O then I was happy,
O then each breath tasted sweeter, and all that day my food
   nourish'd me more, and the beautiful day pass'd well,
And the next came with equal joy, and with the next at
   evening came my friend,
And that night while all was still I heard the waters roll
   slowly continually up the shores,

I heard the hissing rustle of the liquid and sands as directed
    to me whispering to congratulate me,
For the one I love most lay sleeping by me under the same
    cover in the cool night,
In the stillness in the autumn moonbeams his face was
    inclined toward me,
And his arm lay lightly around my breast – and that night I
    was happy.

.

ANONYMOUS

'Shall I Abide this Jesting?'

Shall I abide this jesting?
  I weep, and she's a-feasting.
O cruel fancy that so doth blind thee.
To love one doth not mind thee.

Can I abide this prancing?
  I weep, and she's a-dancing.
O cruel fancy so to betray me,
  Thou goest about to slay me.

SAMUEL BECKETT

from *First Love*

... the name of the woman with whom I was soon to be
united was Lulu. So at least she assured me and I can't see
what interest she could have had in lying to me, on this
score. Of course one can never tell. She also disclosed her
family name, but I've forgotten it. I should have made a
note of it, on a piece of paper, I hate to forget a proper name.
I met her on a bench, on the bank of the canal, one of the
canals, for our town boasts two, though I never knew
which was which. It was a well situated bench, backed by a
mound of solid earth and garbage, so that my rear was
covered. My flanks too, partially, thanks to a pair of
venerable trees, more than venerable, dead, at either end of
the bench. It was no doubt these trees one fine day, aripple
with all their foliage, that had sown the idea of a bench, in
someone's fancy. To the fore, a few yards away, flowed the
canal, if canals flow, don't ask me, so that from that quarter
too the risk of surprise was small. And yet she surprised me.
I lay stretched out, the night being warm, gazing up
through the bare boughs interlocking high above me,
where the trees clung together for support, and through the
drifting cloud, at a patch of starry sky as it came and went.

Shove up, she said. My first movement was to go, but my fatigue, and my having nowhere to go, dissuaded me from acting on it. So I drew back my feet a little way and she sat. Nothing more passed between us that evening and she soon took herself off, without another word. All she had done was sing, beneath her breath, as to herself, and without the words fortunately, some old folk songs, and so disjointedly, skipping from one to another and finishing none, that even I found it strange. The voice, though out of tune, was not unpleasant. It breathed of a soul too soon wearied ever to conclude, that perhaps least arse-aching soul of all. The bench itself was soon more than she could bear and as for me, one look had been enough for her. Whereas in reality she was a most tenacious woman. She came back next day and the day after and all went off more or less as before. Perhaps a few words were exchanged. The next day it was raining and I felt in security. Wrong again. I asked her if she was resolved to disturb me every evening. I disturb you? she said. I felt her eyes on me. They can't have seen much, two eyelids at the most, with a hint of nose and brow, darkly, because of the dark. I thought we were easy, she said. You disturb me, I said, I can't stretch out with you there. The collar of my greatcoat was over my mouth and yet she heard me. Must you stretch out? she said. The mistake one makes is to speak to people. You have only to put your feet on my knees, she said. I didn't wait to be asked twice, under my miserable calves I felt her fat thighs. She began stroking my ankles. You speak to people about stretching out and they immediately see a body at full length. What mattered to me in my dispeopled kingdom, that in regard to which the disposition of my carcass was the merest and most futile of accidents, was supineness in the mind, the dulling of the self and of that residue of execrable frippery known as the

116

non-self and even the world, for short. But man is still today, at the age of twenty-five, at the mercy of an erection, physically too, from time to time, it's the common lot, even I was not immune, if that may be called an erection. It did not escape her naturally, women smell a rigid phallus ten miles away and wonder, How on earth did he spot me from there? One is no longer oneself, on such occasions, and it is painful to be no longer oneself, even more painful if possible than when one is. For when one is one knows what to do to be less so, whereas when one is not one is any old one irredeemably. What goes by the name of love is banishment, with now and then a postcard from the homeland, such is my considered opinion, this evening. When she had finished and my self been resumed, mine own, the mitigable, with the help of a brief torpor, it was alone. I sometimes wonder if that is not all invention, if in reality things did not take quite a different course, one I had no choice but to forget. And yet her image remains bound, for me, to that of the bench, not the bench by day, nor yet the bench by night, but the bench at evening, in such sort that to speak of the bench, as it appeared to me at evening, is to speak of her, for me.

HENRY CAREY

'Sally in Our Alley'

Of all the girls that are so smart
   There's none like pretty Sally;
She is the darling of my heart,
   And she lives in our alley.
There is no lady in the land
   Is half so sweet as Sally;
She is the darling of my heart,
   And she lives in our alley.

Her father he makes cabbage-nets,
   And through the streets does cry 'em;
Her mother she sells laces long
   To such as please to buy 'em:
But sure such folks could ne'er beget
   So sweet a girl as Sally!
She is the darling of my heart,
   And she lives in our alley.

When she is by, I leave my work,
   I love her so sincerely;
My master comes like any Turk,

And bangs me most severely:
But let him bang his bellyful,
　　I'll bear it all for Sally;
She is the darling of my heart,
　　And she lives in our alley.

Of all the days that's in the week
　　I dearly love but one day –
And that's the day that comes betwixt
　　A Saturday and Monday;
For then I'm dressed all in my best
　　To walk abroad with Sally;
She is the darling of my heart,
　　And she lives in our alley.

My master carries me to church,
　　And often am I blamèd
Because I leave him in the lurch
　　As soon as text is namèd;
I leave the church in sermon-time
　　And slink away to Sally;
She is the darling of my heart,
　　And she lives in our alley.

When Christmas comes about again,
　　O, then I shall have money;
I'll hoard it up, and box it all,
　　I'll give it to my honey:
I would it were ten thousand pound,
　　I'd give it all to Sally;
She is the darling of my heart,
　　And she lives in our alley.

My master and the neighbours all,
    Make game of me and Sally,
And, but for her, I'd better be
    A slave and row a galley;
But when my seven long years are out,
    O, then I'll marry Sally;
O, then we'll wed, and then we'll bed –
    But not in our alley!

TADEUSZ KONWICKI

,

from *Bohin Manor*

They took a shortcut back along the forest's edge. The fields were empty of grain and had been partially ploughed. The sky had expanded above the earth and seemed larger than usual. Thrifty squirrels darted among the trees stocking their larders with hazelnuts and acorns.

He took her by the hand. She tried to pull free but he wouldn't let go. Shame kept them both silent, but he was trying to make the best of the situation.

Storks were descending in slow circles in the direction of the river, soon to hold their first parliament before flying off to warmer lands. Helena suddenly recalled the local super-stition – if a young woman sees a stork in a meadow, it means that she'll become pregnant soon. What has happened, she thought. What have I done? But she was in a state of sleepy bliss. I'll think about it later.

He walked alertly beside her. From time to time the sun would break through the thickening clouds and set his hair ablaze, and he would smile tenderly with uncharacteristic timidity.

'We still believe that the sun revolves around the earth. If that's what people thought for thousands of years, it must be so,' she said with sudden gaiety, raising her head.

He bent down and picked up the prickly fruit of a chestnut whose gleaming brown seed casing was visible through a crack. He peeled the chestnut from its green hull and handed it to Helena. She pressed the cold, dazzlingly smooth chestnut to her cheek, which was on fire.

'Give me your hand,' he said softly.

She hesitated for a moment. Elias stood among ferns tall as trees and waited with his hand held out.

'But swear to me that we shall never see each other again.' She placed her hand in his warm palm.

'Why shouldn't we see each other again?'

'We did a terrible thing. God won't forgive us, and neither will people.'

He came to a stop, making her stop too. She could feel the heat emanating from him.

'Come on, this is the end of the nineteenth century. The whole world is out there just waiting for us.'

'My world is here, and it ends here, on the other side of the Ruska Wilderness, by the shore of the Niemen.'

There were wild cumin bushes as tall as palm trees on the fallow in front of them. Once again that strange sound arose from the depths of the earth or the sky. Yes, she thought, my world is coming to an end. My world, our world, is coming to an end again. She had another fit of shivers.

Then he pulled her close to him. She tried to thrust him away, but his dry lips kept kissing a lock of her hair that fluttered in the slight breeze. In fact, he was only touching his lips to her hair, flitting from one place to another like a butterfly. She rested her head against his chest for a moment, then he found her lips and they began a desperate kiss. A cold wing of shadow passed over them. Elias threw his coat on a patch of ground that smelled of summer savory, and they slid slowly down to that bed. She thought she could hear the sound of the church bell in Bujwidze carrying on the wind through the woods – yet another warning.

Then he began forcing his way through her skirts as if through thick branches of young pine. He whispered, requested, explained, but what she heard was the beating of two pulses, her own and his.

'No! No!' she cried in a whisper, and with unexpected strength struggled out from under him and dashed toward the fields. Her feet sank in the freshly turned soil, where crows were already pecking at seed; then she began heading for the woods, breaking into a run when she was in among the cold bushes, yellowing birch leaves, and high anthills.

He raced off in pursuit, certain she was running away forever or would meet with an accident in some forest ravine. She fled in silence and he was afraid to cry out to her. They zigzagged through the forest, sometimes in shadow, sometimes in a downpour of sunlight. Wind-swollen clouds, autumn clouds, clouds born on the shore of the Arctic Sea were racing faster and faster to the northeast in the sky above them.

Finally, she grew tired and stopped by an old pine. Clinging to its black bark, she tried to exhale the immense fatigue lodged in her lungs like dry, spiky pine cones.

Slowing his pace, he pressed his hand to his racing heart and walked slowly over to Helena. They could hear each other breathing now. Slowly, timidly, Elias began to smile.

'Don't be afraid,' he whispered, gasping out the words. 'I'm scared too. We jumped from an awfully high cliff.'

She looked at his forever-blazing hair, his lean face, and

that smile of his, which she knew quite well from some-where but which she couldn't have known from anywhere.

'You know what, you know what?' she said, still short of breath. 'For years I've been having a dream about a huge city with tall buildings, much taller than the ones in Wilno. The trains go under the ground in that city and they make everything shake, they rattle the windows. In the sky over the city, there are balloons with cabins shaped like omnibuses suspended beneath them. People lean out the windows of those cabins and wave white handkerchiefs at the people out strolling the streets of the city. Every dream seems like a continuation of the one before, even though nothing special ever happens in any of them. I'm not running away from anyone, no one's chasing me. No evil forces have cornered me, and there aren't any moments of sudden happiness either. I am just there in that marvellous, unusual city, which exists for me alone and which sends trains under the ground and bright balloons up into the air, all for me.'

'I was gone so long. But you didn't change. Don't you remember me? Don't you remember that Jewish boy who ran with all of his might after your carriage? When his strength was gone, he fell on the heath by the road, trying to catch his breath, as we're doing right now.'

'But I was older than you were,' she said softly and with embarrassment. 'I never paid any attention to adolescents like you.'

'I ran behind you all the way to Krakow, maybe farther.'

He looked at her for a moment, then finally lowered his gaze. Then, quite clumsily, her hands still shaking, she began stroking his hair.

'You're looking at me as if you're saying goodbye,' he said softly.

Not replying, she continued to stroke his hair, and in that gesture there was despair.

'Come on, walk me to the allee. We'll say goodbye there,' she said in a whisper, with a glance up at the sky. 'Christ God, the sun's so low already. What will I tell them at home?'

'You'll have to lie. To lie for my sake.'

They joined hands and walked back along the edge of the woods. I'm doing the same thing people have always done, she thought. Is this the law of nature, òr our own laws of passion? In a minute I'll say goodbye to him forever. And I'll go back; but back to what? To my hermit's freedom, which is no freedom; to Mr Alexander Broel-Plater, who has some horrible secret lurking in his past.

They walked through patches of tall huckleberry ruddy as the ponds at sunset. Helena had to lift her skirt a little. He tried to take her by the arms to carry her to the other side of the patches, but once again she tore free and went on ahead of him.

Now they could hear muffled sounds from the farm. Someone was sawing wood, flails were lashing in one of the barns, the blacksmith was hammering a horseshoe in the smithy behind a clump of willows. They came to a stop at the side of the highroad, not far from where it was joined by the allee at Bohin.

'Don't ever come back,' she said in a whisper. 'What's done is done. Now we have to go back to our lives. You to yours, me to mine.'

'Let's see each other again. Even just once.'

'Don't try to talk me into it. There's no need to see each other again. It'll be easier to part now. Later on it might be too late.'

'Look at me. Didn't God create me to love you?'

She smiled sadly. 'No, go. It's easier this way. You'll forget, and I'll forget too.'

'But I wasn't able to forget all those years. You dreamed about a strange city that doesn't exist on earth. And I dreamed of you. I dreamed of you when I was asleep and when I was on the march, and when I was at sea, when I was awake and when I was delirious with fever.'

'And now it's all come true. Goodbye.'

'It can't be. Everything I did in life was because of you.'

'Don't think badly of me. It has to be this way.'

She began backing away, looking at him with darkening eyes. 'We have to say goodbye.'

'We don't have to. That would be too terrible. It's better that we just part like this. You stay by the road and I'll back away looking at you.'

He was about to reach for her.

'Stop!' she cried in a whisper. 'I'll pray for you.'

'I don't want your prayers,' he said in despair. 'Let's run away to the world together. I'll make boots for a living – I learned how to make beautiful boots – and you'll bring up our children.'

Her smile grew sadder and sadder as she withdrew into the cool dark of the allee. Behind her, by the ponds, was the old maple that had been cleft and felled by lightning, its frighteningly white interior scorched by the flames which the rain had extinguished.

'Farewell. I won't forget you either,' she said quickly, then set off almost at a run toward the manor, feeling his gaze on her trembling shoulders. He remained at the end of the allee and stood there for a long while after she had disappeared on to the porch behind reddening vine leaves.

ANNE BRADSTREET

'To My Dear and Loving Husband'

If ever two were one, then surely we.
If ever man were loved by wife, then thee;
If ever wife was happy in a man,
Compare with me, ye women, if you can.
I prize thy love more than whole mines of gold,
Or all the riches that the east doth hold.
My love is such that rivers cannot quench,
Nor ought but love from thee give recompense.
Thy love is such I can no way repay:
The heavens reward thee manifold, I pray.
Then while we live, in love let's so persévere
That, when we live no more, we may live ever.

SYLVIA TOWNSEND WARNER

from *The Diaries*

11 October 1930

And then we went to bed. Just as I blew out the candle the wind began to rise. I thought I heard her speak, and listened, and at last she said through the door that this would frighten them up at the Vicarage. How the Vicarage led to love I have forgotten (oh, it was an eiderdown). I said, sitting on my side of the wall, that love was easier than liking, so I should specialise in that. 'I think I am utterly loveless.' The forsaken grave wail of her voice smote me, and had me up, and through the door, and at her bedside. There I stayed, till I got into her bed, and found love there, and a confidence that could twit me with how rude I had been the first time we met. We heard a screech-owl wing up the valley to the Vicarage, and after a while it came back to tell us with a few contemptuous hoots, of its errand there.

19 October 1930

She has the stillest face I have ever known. Amusement sharpens it slightly into that fox's smile, but it disdains to smile for pleasure, or turn aside from its melancholy beauty. The loveliest thing of all is how, with bowed head embracing me, her arms and neck pour from those narrow shoulders, like a smooth torrent of water limbed as it falls over a rock.

12 January 1931

It was our most completed night, and after our love I slept unstirring in her arms, still covered with her love, till we woke and ate whatever meal it is lovers eat at five in the morning. She said, remembering Lady C, that Lawrence in heaven would be taken down a peg to see us, specimens of what he so violently disliked, loving according to all his precepts, and perhaps the only lovers that night really to observe them. But heaven would be to be taken down a peg – released from string-strain without displeasure. The body, after all, older and wiser than soul, being first created, and, like a good horse, if given its way would go home by the best path and at the right pace.

V. S. PRITCHETT

❦

from 'The Clerk's Tale'

I was sixteen. The world, the war – I hardly saw or heard of them. The mark of the war on that train meant nothing. I lived in a different world. I lived in a dream. Looking out of the carriage window, sunk in some book, watching the slow clock in the warehouse where I worked, I lived only for one thing in those days: that time should be urged on and the week pass.

So that it would be Sunday once more. For on Sunday, during one hour on Sunday morning, I saw Isabel Hertz. She was in my class at Sunday School, a girl who was half-Swedish, with hair as yellow as thick sunflowers and candid eyes like blue pebbles of ice. Her throat, her lips which broke apart in piety when she sang the hymns, and her silk legs, intoxicated me. Once I fell down the Sunday School stairs when I heard her voice in the doorway below. When she spoke I thought of a crystal of snow falling on a warm hand and instantly melting; a particle of herself melted away with every word and passed with a sigh to Heaven. There, ardent but purified by her purity, I joined her in melodious, fleshless and speechless union. In one of those northern landscapes of snow, perhaps, where time is frozen in the sky, where sleighbells ring and there is the dry mutter of skates saying, 'Inevitable, for ever. Inevitable, for ever,' like our love, over iron lakes of ice.

It was a very small incident which had started my love for Isabel Hertz. It occurred one Sunday at the school. With her Bible on her lap she was sitting opposite to me, for I was afraid to sit next to her.

'Isabel, dear,' the teacher said, 'what is God?' Isabel, who always held her head a little to one side as if her small ears were listening to the spring sky, turned her head. She hesitated, as if waiting for the voice of Heaven; then she replied, 'God is love.'

I was looking at her, waiting for her to speak, and she caught my eye and smiled. A pain like hunger pinched my throat.

All that day I could eat nothing, but my mouth seemed to drink and eat the air because she, miles away, was breathing it. There was a laburnum tree in our garden, and I cut her initials, I.H., on the trunk and went to have a look at them every hour. I even went out after dark before I went to bed and struck a match to see them. I told my parents I had dropped a pencil there and was looking for it. I was awake all night and horses seemed to be galloping over my heart.

I longed to dream at night about Isabel Hertz, but this never happened. I was dreaming about her all day; but when the next Sunday and the next came I felt my body was covered with the garish tattoo of guilt and I could not speak. I never spoke to her. Once when she spoke to me, I choked.

'I Hid My Love'

I hid my love when young till I
Couldn't bear the buzzing of a fly;
I hid my love to my despite
Till I could not bear to look at light:
I dare not gaze upon her face
But left her memory in each place;
Where'er I saw a wild flower lie
I kissed and bade my love good-bye.

I met her in the greenest dells,
Where dewdrops pearl the wood bluebells;
The lost breeze kissed her bright blue eye,
The bee kissed and went singing by,
A sunbeam found a passage there,
A gold chain round her neck so fair;
As secret as the wild bee's song
She lay there all the summer long.

I hid my love in field and town
Till e'en the breeze would knock me down;
The bees seemed singing ballads o'er,

The fly's bass turned a lion's roar;
And even silence found a tongue,
To haunt me all the summer long;
The riddle Nature could not prove
Was nothing else but secret love.

ALBAN BERG

Letter to His Future Wife, Hélène, and Her Reply

Berghof, 23 July 1909

So you *are* angry, Hélène. I write two letters in my anxiety at not hearing from you for three whole days, and I guess you might have fallen out of love with me. And that has made you angry.

Not that there are any angry words in your letter. But what I could read between the lines speaks louder than any angry words. Not a stroke of the pen to suggest any tenderness; no, it gives the impression you regret having worried so much about me and my health. Repelled, no doubt, by my continual moaning and groaning, you leave me to my fate, which amounts to leaving me to rot.

You confess you had another of the horrible times when you were suddenly sick of everything and had to withdraw into yourself. But now everything is all right again, you have become reconciled with life and have found yourself once more. And how was this miracle achieved? Through a glorious summer day with deep blue sky and birds singing. In other words, 'Don't believe I've come back to *you*, Alban. The thing which has rescued and released me and made me immensely happy is not you, with your lamentations of love and your invaid chair, but lovely, heavenly Nature. Now I am myself again, resting in Nature's bosom, which has rescued me from you, Alban, and from my melancholy.'

The rest of the letter discusses the Balzac-Strindberg business in a cool, amiable way – not a straw of love there for a drowning man to cling to. I sit miserably and read right through the letter, considering it from all possible angles, searching for a crumb of comfort, but can only interpret it along the hopeless lines I've just imagined. Perhaps you wrote the letter in your first irritation, but surely you can understand how hurt I would be on getting it, the first letter I've had from you for three days.

Listen, Hélène, I know I've written too much about my illness. But it wasn't just whining and whimpering, I wanted to let you know how hard I've been trying to get well, and that I was in despair of ever getting well in this damned place; especially of ever getting well without *you*. Oh, they feed me up here, but it's more than cancelled out by my lack of emotional nourishment, my continual craving for *you*. And now you seem to be telling me plainly: 'I relieve you of your promise, live as you wish' – in other words: 'I don't care if you go to pieces.'

Oh, Hélène, why are you doing this to me? With your blue sky and bird-song have you forgotten our last days together? The Wachau, the terrace garden, the journey? I thought you were thinking of all these things, but instead you have completely forgotten them, and feel released and rescued and immensely happy, just because the sun is shining. I can't expect you not to enjoy Nature because I'm not there; perhaps no woman can love as fully as that. But I am hurt, more than I can say, to find you can quite do without me because you enjoy Nature. Imagine my despondency and despair, knowing that every shining

135

cloud will put me in the shade, every warbling nightingale, every trilling lark will drown the cry of longing. Imagine how I must stagger and stumble around if your hand is not outstretched to hold mine, because it rests contentedly in the moss and plays in the grass. If you have no eyes for me, but only for the swaying branches in the forest . . .

I must get to you, I can't be without you any more. You'll get this letter on Monday, so I may have news on Tuesday, and will let you know when and where I'll be coming. And plase send me a loving word, so that I'll have something to hope for in these three days, and to live on afterwards: until I lie at your feet, to be trampled on, or lifted up.

Alban

Trahütten, 23 July 1909

Alban dear,

When my letter to you had gone yesterday, I was sorry, because I hadn't been quite honest. I was trying, by rather drastic means, to force you into considering what may happen if you don't soon restore your health. I'm sure it must have suffered a good deal from the effects of your not living in a more sensible way. Look, it's all right for Smaragda to drag you off with her carousing all night, and Hermann does the same when he's in Europe. But she has a good long sleep next day, whereas you get up without enough sleep and try to work, fighting your tiredness by drinking all those cups of strong tea. And what with these nights in smoky places, with alcohol and no food, you've reached the point of being nearly six foot tall and weighing only 9½ stone. I can well understand your hating all the 'fattening food', but it's still the most harmless way of growing stronger, instead of taking medicines the whole time without their making you any better.

These last days I've been very unhappy about all this. You are always writing of your great love for me, but you don't seem to care that our future depends on your health improving. From their point of view, my parents aren't altogether wrong to turn you down. They think I should be constantly worrying about you and so wouldn't be happy with you. Any woman who loves is bound to wonder whether her love is going to bring her suffering, even though it may be her destiny to suffer. But won't *you*, Alban, have one more try to get well? It will take some sacrifices, I admit, but surely you will want to do it for my sake – no, for *our* sakes.

I've had a bad night, because I knew my letter would hurt you, saying harsh things to you, as if I weren't interested any more in you and your health. But no, Alban, I am *not* giving you up. Perhaps you will still achieve something 'great' one day, and I want to help you with it, so that you can do your work unhampered by physical frailty, and can also enjoy life without having heart trouble and attacks of asthma.

So that's that, a long long sermon, and a confession too. Take it as it's meant, and please – be patient.

Your own
Hélène

W. H. AUDEN

'Appletreewick'

Fair land where all is brave and kind
Thy face is often in my mind
Where heather may be always seen
And there is grass that's really green
Where trees remember how to dance
And squirrels peep through every branch.
The birds will sit on nests they've made
Still as you pass all unafraid.
Where all the flowers have mossy thrones
And streams play hide and seek with stones
Or make each mill a spinning top
Blowing big bubbles as they drop.
Clouds chase each other in blue skies
And throw their shadows in our eyes
Where one can walk for miles and miles
And meet with neither gate nor stiles
Where cottages are small and white
Their windows shine like stars at night.
And there are inns where one can go
And meet the finest men I know.
There one can sit by blazing fires

Can smoke and talk for hours and hours
Of harvesting, of sheep, of carts,
To men with simple lovely hearts.
Fare well. I hear in my day-dreams
The laughter of thy woods and streams.
Thy hills must now be white with snow
But whiter is thy heart, I know.

WILLIAM SHAKESPEARE

♥

from *The Winter's Tale*

FLORIZEL   What you do
Still betters what is done. When you speak, sweet,
I'ld have you do it ever. When you sing,
I'ld have you buy and sell so, so give alms,
Pray so, and for the ord'ring your affairs,
To sing them too. When you do dance, I wish you
A wave o' th' sea, that you might ever do
Nothing but that, move still, still so,
And own no other function. Each your doing,
So singular in each particular,
Crowns what you are doing in the present deeds,
That all your acts are queens.

PERDITA   O Doricles,
Your praises are too large. But that your youth,
And the true blood which peeps fairly through't,
Do plainly give you out an unstained shepherd,
With wisdom I might fear, my Doricles,
You wooed me the false way.

FLORIZEL   I think you have
  As little skill to fear as I have purpose
  To put you to't. But come; our dance, I pray.
  Your hand, my Perdita. So turtles pair
  That never mean to part.

GABRIEL   GARCIA   MARQUEZ

❦

from *Love in the Time of Cholera*

Florentino Ariza was one of the few who stayed until the
funeral was over. He was soaked to the skin and returned
home terrified that he would catch pneumonia after so
many years of meticulous care and excessive precautions.
He prepared hot lemonade with a shot of brandy, drank it in
bed with two aspirin tablets, and, wrapped in a wool
blanket, sweated by the bucketful until the proper equil-
ibrium had been re-established in his body. When he
returned to the wake he felt his vitality completely restored.
Fermina Daza had once again assumed command of the
house, which was cleaned and ready to receive visitors, and
on the altar in the library she had placed a portrait in pastels
of her dead husband, with a black border around the frame.
By eight o'clock there were as many people and as intense a
heat as the night before, but after the rosary someone
circulated the request that everyone leave early so that the
widow could rest for the first time since Sunday afternoon.

Fermina Daza said goodbye to most of them at the altar,
but she accompanied the last group of intimate friends to
the street door so that she could lock it herself, as she had
always done, as she was prepared to do with her final

breath, when she saw Florentino Ariza, dressed in mourning and standing in the middle of the deserted drawing room. She was pleased, because for many years she had erased him from her life, and this was the first time she saw him clearly, purified by forgetfulness. But before she could thank him for the visit, he placed his hat over his heart, tremulous and dignified, and the abscess that had sustained his life finally burst.

'Fermina,' he said, 'I have waited for this opportunity for more than half a century, to repeat to you once again my vow of eternal fidelity and everlasting love.'

Fermina Daza would have thought she was facing a madman if she had not had reason to believe that at that moment Florentino Ariza was inspired by the grace of the Holy Spirit. Her first impulse was to curse him for profaning the house when the body of her husband was still warm in the grave. But the dignity of her fury held her back. 'Get out of here,' she said. 'And don't show your face again for the years of life that are left to you.' She opened the street door, which she had begun to close, and concluded:

'And I hope there are very few of them.'

When she heard his steps fade away in the deserted street she closed the door very slowly with the crossbar and the locks, and faced her destiny alone. Until that moment she had never been fully conscious of the weight and size of the drama that she had provoked when she was not yet eighteen, and that would pursue her until her death. She wept for the first time since the afternoon of the disaster, without witnesses, which was the only way she wept. She wept for the death of her husband, for her solitude and rage, and when she went into the empty bedroom she wept for herself because she had rarely slept alone in that bed since the loss of her virginity. Everything that belonged to her husband made her weep again: his tasselled slippers, his pyjamas under the pillow, the space of his absence in the dressing table mirror, his own odour on her skin. A vague thought made her shudder: 'The people one loves should take all their things with them when they die.' She did not want anyone's help to get ready for bed, she did not want to eat anything before she went to sleep. Crushed by grief, she prayed to God to send her death that night while she slept, and with that hope she lay down, barefoot but fully dressed, and fell asleep on the spot. She slept without realising it, but she knew in her sleep that she was still alive, and that she had half a bed to spare, that she was lying on her left side on the left-hand side of the bed as she always did, but that she missed the weight of the other body on the other side. Thinking as she slept, she thought that she would never again be able to sleep this way, and she began to sob in her sleep, and she slept, sobbing, without changing position on her side of the bed, until long after the roosters crowed and she was awakened by the despised sun of the morning without him. Only then did she realise that she had slept a long time without dying, sobbing in her sleep, and that while she slept, sobbing, she had thought more about Florentino Ariza than about her dead husband.

HENRY CLOUD

from *Barbara Cartland: Crusader in Pink*

Not that she really had to worry. She was enjoying life. The Twenties life of London was already in full swing, and Barbara was making the most of it with true Cartland gusto, still falling in and out of love with a succession of penniless and honourable young men, still turning down proposals left and right, still dancing until dawn, and still – incredible though it must seem today – preserving her virginity. 'In those days I did not even know what deep passionate kissing was,' she says. 'When I did learn many years later I was shocked.'

She became engaged – then disengaged. One suitor actually produced his officer's revolver in a taxi (an interesting period touch) and threatened to kill himself if she refused to marry him. Even this failed to sway her, and she relied increasingly on Polly now who had developed practised expertise in calming down her daughter's rejected suitors. The young man wept on Polly's shoulder, the threatened suicide did not take place, and Barbara bounced on through her early twenties, Park Gates and unwed Dukes apparently as far away as ever.

ETHEL M. DELL

from *Greatheart*

A great shiver went through him; he gripped his hands together suddenly and passionately.

'O my God,' he groaned, 'it's the hardest thing on earth – to stand and do nothing – when I love her so!'

Something seemed to give way within him with the words. His shoulders shook convulsively. He buried his face in his arms.

And in that moment the power that had stayed Dinah upon the threshold suddenly urged her forward.

Almost before she realised it she was there at his side, stooping over him, holding him – holding him fast in a clasp that was free from any hesitation or fear, a clasp in which all her pulsing womanhood rushed forth to him, exulting, glorying in its self-betrayal.

'My dear! Oh, my dear!' she said. 'Are you praying for me?'

'Dinah!' he said.

Just her name, no more, but spoken in a tone that thrilled her through and through! He leaned against her for a few moments, almost as if he feared to move. Then, as one gathering strength, he uttered a great sigh and slowly got to his feet.

'You mustn't bother about me,' he said, and the sudden rapture had all gone out of his voice; it had the flatness of utter weariness. 'I shall be all right.'

But Dinah's hands yet clung to his shoulders. Those moments of yielding had revealed to her more than any subsequent word or action could belie. Her eyes, shining with a great light, looked straight into his.

'Dear Scott! Dear Greatheart!' she said, and her voice trembled over the tender utterance of the name. 'Are you in trouble? Can't I help?'

He took her face between his hands, looking straight back into the shining eyes. 'You are the trouble, Dinah,' he told her simply. 'And I'd give all I have – I'd give my soul – to make life easier for you.'

She leaned towards him, and suddenly those shining eyes were blurred with a glimmer of tears. 'Life is dreadfully difficult,' she said. 'But you have never done anything but help me. And, oh, Scott, I – don't know if I ought to tell you – forgive me if it's wrong – but – but I feel I must!' – her breath came so quickly that she could hardly utter the words – 'I love you – I love you – better than any one else in the world!'

'Dinah!' he said, as one incredulous.

'It's true!' she panted. 'It's true! Eustace knows it – has known it almost as long as I have. It isn't the only thing I have to tell you, but it's the first – and biggest. And even though – even though – I shall never be anything more to you than I am now – I'm glad – I'm proud – for you to know. There's nothing else that counts in the same way. And though – though I refused you the other day – I wanted you – dreadfully, dreadfully. If – if I had only been good enough for you, – but – but – I'm not!' She broke off, battling with herself.

147

He was still holding her face between his hands, and there was something of insistence, something that even bordered upon ruthlessness, in his hold. Though the tears were running down her face, he would not let her go.

'Will you tell me what you mean by that?' he said, his voice very low. 'Or – must I ask Eustace?'

She started. There was that in his tone that made her wince inexplicably. 'Oh no,' she said, 'no! I'll tell you myself – if – if you must know.'

'I am afraid I must,' he said, and for all their resolution, the words had a sound of deadly weariness. He let her go slowly as he uttered them. 'Sit down!' he said gently. 'And please don't tremble! There is nothing to make you afraid.'

She dropped into the chair he indicated, and made a desperate effort to calm herself. He stood beside her with the absolute patience of one accustomed to long waiting.

After a few moments, she put up a quivering hand, seeking his. He took it instantly, and as his fingers closed firmly upon her own, she found courage.

'I didn't want you to know,' she whispered. 'But I – I see now – it's better that you should. There's no other way – of making you understand. It's just this – just this!' She swallowed hard, striving to control the piteous trembling of her voice. 'I am – one of those people – that – that never ought to have been born. I don't belong – anywhere – except to – my mother, who – who – who has no use for me – hated me before ever I came into the world. You see, she – married because – because – another man – my real father – had played her false. Oh! do you wonder – do you wonder' – she bowed her forehead upon his hand with a rush of tears – 'that – that when I knew – I – I felt as if – I couldn't – go on with life?'

Her weeping was piteous; it shook her from head to foot.

But – in the very midst of her distress – there came to her a wonder so great that it checked her tears at the height of their flow. For very suddenly it dawned upon her that Scott – Scott, her knight of the golden armour – was kneeling at her feet.

Half in wonder and half in awe, she lifted her head and looked at him. And in that moment he took her two hands and kissed them, tenderly, reverently, lingeringly.

'Was this what you and Eustace were talking about this afternoon?' he said.

She nodded. 'I had to tell him – why – I couldn't marry you. He – he had been – so kind.'

'But, my own Dinah,' he said, and in his voice was a quiver half-quizzical yet strangely charged with emotion, 'did you ever seriously imagine that I should allow a sordid little detail like that to come between us? Surely Eustace knew better than that!'

She heard him in amazement, scarcely believing that she heard. 'Do you – can you mean,' she faltered, 'that – it really – doesn't count?'

'I mean that it is less than nothing to me,' he made answer, and in his eyes as they looked into hers was that glory of worship that she had once seen in a dream. 'I mean, my darling, that since you want me as I want you, nothing – nothing in the world – can ever come between us any more. Oh, my dear, my dear, I wish you'd told me sooner.'

'I knew I ought to,' she murmured, still hardly believing. 'And yet – somehow – I couldn't bear the thought of your knowing – particularly as – as – till Eustace told me – I never dreamed you – cared. You are so – great. You ought to have someone so much – better than I. I'm not nearly good enough – not nearly.'

He was drawing her to him, and she went with a little sob into his arms; but she turned her face away over his shoulder, avoiding his.

'I ought not – to have told you – I loved you,' she said brokenly. 'It wasn't right of me. Only – when I saw you so unhappy – I couldn't – somehow – keep it in any longer. Dear Scott, don't you think – before – before we go any farther – you had better – forget it and – give me up?'

'No, I don't think so.' Scott spoke very softly, with the utmost tenderness, into her ear. 'Don't you realise,' he said, 'that we belong to each other? Could there possibly be anyone else for either you or me?'

She did not answer him; only she clung a little closer. And, after a moment, as she felt the drawing of his hold, 'Don't kiss me – yet!' she begged him tremulously. 'Let us wait till – the morning!'

His arms relaxed. 'It is very near the morning now,' he said. 'Shall we go and watch for it?'

They rose together. Dinah's eyes sought his for one shy, fleeting second, falling instantly as if half-dazzled, half-afraid. He took her hand and led her quietly from the room.

It was no longer dark in the passage outside. A pearly light was growing. The splash of the sea sounded very far below them, as the dim surging of a world unseen might rise to the watchers on the mountain-top.

WILLIAM PLOMER

'The Widow's Plot'
or 'She Got What Was Coming to Her'

Troubled was a house in Ealing
Where a widow's only son
Found her fond maternal feeling
    Overdone.

She was fussy and possessive;
Lennie, in his teens,
Found the atmosphere oppressive;
    There were scenes.

Tiring one day of her strictures
Len went down the street,
Took a ticket at the pictures,
    Took his seat.

The picture was designed to thrill
But oh, the girl he sat beside!
If proximity could kill
    He'd have died.

Simple, sweet, sixteen and blonde,
Unattached, her name was Bess.
Well, boys, how would *you* respond?
    I can guess.

Len and Bessie found each other
All that either could desire,
But the fat, when he told Mother,
    Was in the fire.

The widow, who had always dreaded
This might happen, hatched a scheme
To smash, when they were duly wedded,
    Love's young dream.

One fine day she murmured, 'Sonny,
It's not for me to interfere,
You may think it rather funny
    But I hear

'Bess goes out with other men.'
'I don't believe it! It's a lie!
Tell me who with, where, and when?
    Tell me why?'

'Keep cool, Lennie. I suspected
That the girl was far from nice.
What a pity you rejected
    My advice.'

Suspicion from this fatal seed
Sprang up overnight
And strangled, like a poisonous weed,
    The lilies of delight.

Still unbelieving, Len believed
That Bess was being unchaste,
And a man that feels himself deceived
    May act in haste.

Now Bess was innocence incarnate
And never thought of other men;
She visited an aunt at Barnet
    Now and then,

But mostly stayed at home and dusted,
Crooning early, crooning late,
Unaware of being distrusted
    By her mate.

Then one day a wire was sent:
MEET ME PALACEUM AT EIGHT
URGENT AUNTIE. Bessie went
    To keep the date.

Slightly anxious, Bessie came
To the unusual rendezvous.
Desperate, Lennie did the same,
    He waited too,

Seeing but unseen by Bessie,
And in a minute seeing red –
For a stranger, fat and dressy,
    A trilby on his head,

In his tie a tasteful pearl,
On his face a nasty leer,
Sidled up towards the girl
    And called her 'Dear'.

At this juncture Len stepped in,
Made a bee-line for the lout,
With a straight left to the chin
    Knocked him out.

He might have done the same for Bess
Thinking still that she had tricked him,
But she was gazing in distress
    At the victim.

'It's a *her*!' she cried (but grammar
Never was her strongest suit):
'She's passed out!' he heard her stammer,
    'Lennie, scoot!'

'It's *what*? A *her*? Good God, it's *Mum*!'
Ah, now I see! A wicked plan
To make me think my Bess had come
    To meet a *man* – '

'Now what's all this?' a copper said,
Shoving the crowd aside. 'I heard a
Rumour somebody was dead.
    Is it murder?'

Len quite candidly replied,
'No, officer, it's something less.
It's justifiable matricide,
    Isn't it, Bess?'

JAMES JOYCE

♪

from 'The Dead' in *Dubliners*

– Gretta dear, what are you thinking about?

She did not answer nor yield wholly to his arm. He said again, softly:

– Tell me what it is, Gretta. I think I know what is the matter. Do I know?

She did not answer at once. Then she said in an outburst of tears:

– O, I am thinking about that song, 'The Lass of Aughrim'.

She broke loose from him and ran to the bed and, throwing her arms across the bed-rail, hid her face. Gabriel stood stock-still for a moment in astonishment and then followed her. As he passed in the way of the cheval-glass he caught sight of himself in full length, his broad, well-filled shirt-front, the face whose expression always puzzled him when he saw it in a mirror and his glimmering gilt-rimmed eye-glasses. He halted a few paces from her and said:

– What about the song? Why does that make you cry?

She raised her head from her arms and dried her eyes with the back of her hand like a child. A kinder note than he had intended went into his voice.

– Why, Gretta? he asked.

– I am thinking about a person long ago who used to sing that song.

– And who was the person long ago? asked Gabriel, smiling.

– It was a person I used to know in Galway when I was living with my grandmother, she said.

The smile passed away from Gabriel's face. A dull anger began to gather again at the back of his mind and the dull fires of his lust began to glow angrily in his veins.

– Someone you were in love with? he asked ironically.

– It was a young boy I used to know, she answered, named Michael Furey. He used to sing that song, 'The Lass of Aughrim'. He was very delicate.

Gabriel was silent. He did not wish her to think that he was interested in this delicate boy.

– I can see him so plainly, she said after a moment. Such eyes as he had: big dark eyes! And such an expression in them – an expression!

– O then, you were in love with him? said Gabriel.

– I used to go out walking with him, she said, when I was in Galway.

A thought flew across Gabriel's mind.

– Perhaps that was why you wanted to go to Galway with that Ivors girl? he said coldly.

She looked at him and asked in surprise:

– What for?

Her eyes made Gabriel feel awkward. He shrugged his shoulders and said:

– How do I know? To see him perhaps.

She looked away from him along the shaft of light towards the window in silence.

– He is dead, she said at length. He died when he was

only seventeen. Isn't it a terrible thing to die so young as that?'

– What was he? asked Gabriel, still ironically.

– He was in the gasworks, she said.

Gabriel felt humiliated by the failure of his irony and by the evocation of this figure from the dead, a boy in the gasworks. While he had been full of memories of their secret life together, full of tenderness and joy and desire, she had been comparing him in her mind with another. A shameful consciousness of his own person assailed him. He saw himself as a ludicrous figure, acting as a pennyboy for his aunts, a nervous well-meaning sentimentalist, orating to vulgarians and idealising his own clownish lusts, the pitiable fatuous fellow he had caught a glimpse of in the mirror. Instinctively he turned his back more to the light lest she might see the shame that burned upon his forehead.

He tried to keep up his tone of cold interrogation but his voice when he spoke was humble and indifferent.

– I suppose you were in love with this Michael Furey, Gretta, he said.

– I was great with him at that time, she said.

Her voice was veiled and sad. Gabriel, feeling now how vain it would be to try to lead her whither he had purposed, caressed one of her hands and said, also sadly:

– And what did he die of so young, Gretta? Consumption, was it?

– I think he died for me, she answered.

A vague terror seized Gabriel at this answer as if, at that hour when he had hoped to triumph, some impalpable and vindictive being was coming against him, gathering forces against him in its vague world. But he shook himself free of it with an effort of reason and continued to caress her hand. He did not question her again for he felt that she would tell

157

him of herself. Her hand was warm and moist: it did not respond to his touch but he continued to caress it just as he had caressed her first letter to him that spring morning.

– It was in the winter, she said, about the beginning of the winter when I was going to leave my grandmother's and come up here to the convent. And he was ill at the time in his lodgings in Galway and wouldn't be let out and his people in Oughterard were written to. He was in decline, they said, or something like that. I never knew rightly.

She paused for a moment and sighed.

– Poor fellow, she said. He was very fond of me and he was such a gentle boy. We used to go out together, walking, you know, Gabriel, like the way they do in the country. He was going to study singing only for his health. He had a very good voice, poor Michael Furey.

– Well; and then? asked Gabriel.

– And then when it came to the time for me to leave Galway and come up to the convent he was much worse and I wouldn't be let see him so I wrote a letter saying I was going up to Dublin and would be back in the summer and hoping he would be better then.

She paused for a moment to get her voice under control and then went on:

– Then the night before I left I was in my grandmother's house in Nuns' Island, packing up, and I heard gravel thrown up against the window. The window was so wet I couldn't see so I ran downstairs as I was and slipped out the back into the garden and there was the poor fellow at the end of the garden, shivering.

– And did you not tell him to go back? asked Gabriel.

– I implored of him to go home at once and told him he would get his death in the rain. But he said he did not want to live. I can see his eyes as well as well! He was standing at the end of the wall where there was a tree.

– And did he go home? asked Gabriel.

– Yes, he went home. And when I was only a week in the convent he died and he was buried in Oughterard where his people came from. O, the day I heard that, that he was dead!

She stopped, choking with sobs, and, overcome by emotion, flung herself face downward on the bed, sobbing in the quilt. Gabriel held her hand for a moment longer, irresolutely, and, then, shy of intruding on her grief, let it fall gently and walked quietly to the window.

FERNANDO PESSOA

♥

'Chance'

In the chance of the street the chance of the blonde girl,
But no, it is not her.

The other was in the other street, in the other town, and I
    was someone else.

I am suddenly lost in the immediate vision.
Another time I am in the other town, in the other street,
And the other girl goes by.

What a great advantage to recall without compromise!
Now I am sorry I have never seen the other girl,
And I am sorry I have not after all so much as looked her
    way.

What a great adventure to wear your soul turned inside
    out!
At least poetry gets written.
Poetry gets written, you pass for mad, and then for a
    genius, probably,
Probably, or even improbably,
A marvel among celebrities!

I was saying that at least poetry gets written . . .
But that was regarding a girl,
A blonde girl,
But which one?

There was one I saw long ago in another town,
In another sort of street;
And there was the one I saw long ago in another town
In another sort of street;
For all memories are the same memory,·
Everything that was is the same death,
Yesterday, today, who knows about tomorrow?

A passer-by looks my way for moment puzzled.
Could I be making poetry in gestures and faces?
Maybe . . . The blonde girl?
It is the same one after all . . .
Everything is the same after all . . .

Only I, somehow, am not the same, and that is the same too
    after all.

ALICE MUNRO

from 'The Beggar Maid'

She could not turn Patrick down. She could not do it. It was not the amount of money but the amount of love he offered that she could not ignore; she believed that she felt sorry for him, that she had to help him out. It was as if he had come up to her in a crowd carrying a large, simple, dazzling object – a huge egg, maybe, of solid silver, something of doubtful use and punishing weight – and was offering it to her, in fact thrusting it at her, begging her to take some of the weight of it off him. If she thrust it back, how could he bear it? But that explanation left something out. It left out her own appetite, which was not for wealth but for worship. The size, the weight, the shine, of what he said was love (and she did not doubt him) had to impress her, even though she had never asked for it. It did not seem likely such an offering would come her way again. Patrick himself, though worshipful, did in some oblique way acknowledge her luck.

She had always thought this would happen, that somebody would look at her and love her totally and helplessly. At the same time she had thought that nobody would, nobody would want her at all, and up until now nobody had. What made you wanted was nothing you did, it was something you had, and how could you ever tell whether you had it? She would look at herself in the glass and think: Wife, sweetheart. Those mild lovely words. How could they apply to her? It was a miracle; it was a mistake. It was what she had dreamed of; it was not what she wanted.

She grew very tired, irritable, sleepless. She tried to think admiringly of Patrick. His lean, fair-skinned face was really very handsome. He must know a number of things. He graded papers, presided at examinations, he was finishing his thesis. There was a smell of pipe tobacco and rough wool about him that she liked. He was twenty-four. No other girl she knew who had a boyfriend had one as old as that.

Then without warning she thought of him saying, 'I suppose I don't seem very manly.' She thought of him saying, 'Do you love me? Do you really love me?' He would look at her in a scared and threatening way. Then when she said yes he said how lucky he was, how lucky they were; he mentioned friends of his and their girls, comparing their love affairs unfavourably to his and Rose's. Rose would shiver with irritation and misery. She was sick of herself as much as him, she was sick of the picture they made at this moment, walking across a snowy downtown park, her bare hand snuggled in Patrick's, in his pocket. Some outrageous and cruel things were being shouted inside her. She had to do something, to keep them from getting out. She started tickling and teasing him.

Outside Dr Henshawe's back door, in the snow, she kissed him, tried to make him open his mouth, she did scandalous things to him. When he kissed her his lips were soft; his tongue was shy; he collapsed over rather than held her, she could not find any force in him.

'You're lovely. You have lovely skin. Such fair eyebrows. You're so delicate.'

She was pleased to hear that, anybody would be. But she said warningly, 'I'm not so delicate, really. I'm quite large.'

'You don't know how I love you. There's a book I have called *The White Goddess*. Every time I look at the title it reminds me of you.'

She wriggled away from him. She bent down and got a handful of snow from the drift by the steps and clapped it on his head.

'My White God.'

He shook the snow out. She scooped up some more and threw it at him. He didn't laugh; he was surprised and alarmed. She brushed the snow off his eyebrows and licked it off his ears. She was laughing, though she felt desperate rather than merry. She didn't know what made her do this.

from *My Father and Myself*

It is, for me, the interesting part of this personal history that peace and contentment reached me in the shape of an animal, an Alsatian bitch. Is it, I wonder, of any value as a clue to my psychology to recall that in my play *The Prisoners of War* the hero, Captain Conrad (myself of course), unable to build on human relations, takes to a plant? He tells some story of another imprisoned officer who fell in love with a pet rabbit and read short stories to it out of a magazine. 'Plants or rabbits,' he says, 'it's the same thing.' This bitch of mine entered my life in the middle forties and entirely transformed it. I have already described her in two books; it is necessary to say here that I don't believe there was anything special about her, except that she was rather a beauty. In this context it is not she herself but her effect upon me that I find interesting. She offered me what I had never found in my sexual life, constant, single-hearted, incorruptible, uncritical devotion, which it is in the nature of dogs to offer. She placed herself entirely under my control. From the moment she established herself in my heart and home, my obsession with sex fell wholly away from me. The pubs I had spent so much of my time in were never revisited, my single desire was to get back to her, to her waiting love and unstaling welcome. So urgent was my longing every day to rejoin her that I would often take taxis part-way, even the whole way, home to Putney from my London office, rather than endure the dawdling of buses and the rush-hour traffic jams in Park Lane. I sang with joy at the thought of seeing her. I never prowled the London streets again, nor had the slightest inclination to do so. On the contrary, whenever I thought of it, I was positively thankful to be rid of it all, the anxieties, the frustrations, the wastage of time and spirit. It was as though I had never wanted sex at all, and that this extraordinary long journey of mine which had seemed a pursuit of it had really been an attempt to escape from it. I was just under fifty when this animal came into my hands, and the fifteen years she lived with me were the happiest of my life.

E. J. SCOVELL

'In a Wood'

I saw my love, younger than primroses,
Sleeping in a wood.
Why do I love best what sleep uncloses,
Sorrowful creaturehood?

Dark, labyrinthine with anxiety,
His face is like coiled infancy;
Like parched and wrinkled buds, the first of the year,
Thrown out on winter air.

Stiller than close eyes of a nested bird,
Clear from the covert of his sleeping,
One looked out that knows no human word
But gives me love and weeping.

TADEUSZ BOROWSKI

from *This Way for the Gas, Ladies and Gentlemen*

You know, it feels very strange to be writing to you, you whose face I have not seen for so long. At times I can barely remember what you look like – your image fades from my memory despite my efforts to recall it. And yet my dreams about you are incredibly vivid; they have an almost physical reality. A dream, you see, is not necessarily visual. It may be an emotional experience in which there is depth and where one feels the weight of an object and the warmth of a body . . .

It is hard for me to imagine you on a prison bunk, with your hair shaved off after the typhoid fever. I see you still as I saw you the last time at the Pawiak prison: a tall, willowy young woman with sad eyes and a gentle smile. Later, at the Gestapo headquarters, you sat with your head bent low, so I could see nothing but your black hair that has now been shaven off.

And this is what has remained most vivid in my memory: this picture of you, even though I can no longer clearly recall your face. And that is why I write you such long letters – they are our evening talks, like the ones we used to have on Staryszewska Street. And that is why my letters are not sad. I have kept my spirit and I know that you have not lost yours either. Despite everything. Despite your hidden face at the Gestapo headquarters, despite the typhoid fever, despite the pneumonia – and despite the shaved head . . .

. . . I am thinking about Staryszewska Street. I look at the dark window, at my face reflected in the glass, and outside I see the blackness occasionally broken by the sudden flash of the watch-tower searchlight that silhouettes fragments of objects in the dark. I look into the night and I think of Staryszewska Street. I remember the sky, pale and luminous, and the bombed-out house across the street. I think of how much I longed for your body during those days, and I often smile to myself imagining the consternation after my arrest when they must have found in my room, next to my books and my poems, your perfume and your robe, heavy and red like the brocades in Velazquez's paintings.

I think of how very mature you were; what devotion and – forgive me if I say it now – selflessness you brought to our love, how graciously you used to walk into my life which offered you nothing but a single room without plumbing, evenings with cold tea, a few wilting flowers, a dog that was always playfully gnawing at your shoes, and a paraffin lamp.

I think about these things and smile condescendingly when people speak to me of morality, of law, of tradition, of obligation . . . Or when they discard all tenderness and sentiment and, shaking their fists, proclaim this the age of toughness. I smile and I think that one human being must always be discovering another – through love. And that this is the most important thing on earth, and the most lasting.

GAVIN EWART

The Lover Writes a One-Word Poem

YOU!

WILLIAM SHAKESPEARE

♪

Sonnet 104

To me fair friend you never can be old,
For as you were when first your eye I eyed,
Such seems your beauty still: three winters cold,
Have from the forests shook three summers' pride,
Three beauteous springs to yellow autumn turned,
In process of the seasons have I seen,
Three April perfumes in three hot Junes burned,
Since first I saw you fresh which yet are green.
Ah yet doth beauty like a dial hand,
Steal from his figure, and no pace perceived,
So your sweet hue, which methinks still doth stand
Hath motion, and mine eye may be deceived.
    For fear of which, hear this thou age unbred,
    Ere you were born was beauty's summer dead.

ACKNOWLEDGEMENTS

The editor and publishers wish to thank the following for permission to use copyright material:

Calder Publications Ltd for an extract from Samuel Beckett, *First Love* (1970) Calder & Boyars, pp. 19–25;

Carcanet Press Ltd for E. J. Scovell, 'In a Wood' from *Collected Poems* (1988); and Fernando Pessoa, 'Chance', trans. Keith Bosley, from *A Collected Pessoa*, eds. Eugenio Lisboa and L. C. Taylor (1995);

Faber & Faber Ltd for W. H. Auden, 'Appletreewick' from *Juvenilia Poems 1922–1928*, ed. Katherine Bucknell (1994); with Farrar, Straus & Giroux, Inc. for Robert Lowell, 'The Old Lady's Lament for Her Youth' from *Imitations*. © 1959 by Robert Lowell, renewed © 1987 by Harriet Lowell, Sheridan Lowell and Caroline Lowell; Ezra Pound, 'The River-merchant's Wife: A Letter' from *Collected Shorter Poems* (1926); and extracts from Alban Berg, *Letters to His Wife*, trans. Bernard Grun (1971) pp. 68–70; and with Farrar, Straus & Giroux, Inc. for Tadeusz Konwicki, *Bohin Manor*, trans. Richard Lourie. Translation © 1990 by Farrar, Straus & Giroux, Inc.;

Victor Gollancz Ltd for an extract from *The Memoirs of Hector Berlioz*, trans. and ed. David Calms (1969) pp. 214–7;

David Higham Associates on behalf of the Estate of the author

CHILDHOOD · FRIENDSHIP · FIRS